DIE FOR ME DARLING

PSYCHOLOGICAL THRILLER

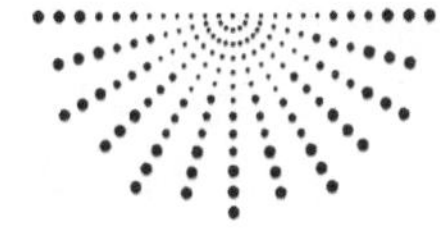

CAROLINE CLARK

CAZCLARK.COM

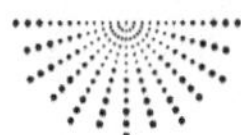

The paper felt like silk in Nick's hand, yet it was so much more. With a lump in his throat, the room shrunk down, and all that existed was the five by seven glossy print he held in his shaking hand. Would he ever hold his own photo? Would he ever be able to stand there like John, chest out a big goofy grin on his face, showing the world his pride, his joy, his creation? Nick swallowed and let his eyes devour every detail. The chubby cheeks that were formed into a smile. The blue eyes so deep you wondered if they were real and the tiny fingers, so small yet so perfectly formed they made him want to cry with joy. Involuntarily he reached out to hold that hand, and a wave of disappointment crushed him as he touched paper.

"She's so beautiful," Nick managed through a throat that felt as dry as sandpaper and just as brittle. He wanted to ask more, but a lump had formed behind his Adam's apple, and no words could squeeze past as it filled him with despair and pushed moisture to the back of his eyes. Blinking up at John, he handed the photo back.

"Alice," John said, clutching it to his chest. "We called her Alice. She was seven pounds exactly, and it was the easiest birth the midwife had seen in over a year."

Nick could hear the words, but they seemed to be coming from so far away that he had to focus hard to understand them. For a second, the room went black, and he thought he would fall to the ground. *Get a grip.* He should be pleased for his mate, not devastated that once again, he stood on the outside as one more of his friends showed off their latest progeny.

"She's beautiful," he said again, and then he turned away quickly before John could spot the tears that pricked at the back of his eyes. "I'll see you tomorrow, mate."

Nick picked up his briefcase and made his way to the lift. Once the doors closed behind him, he leaned against the wall and let the shakes come as he was whisked down the twenty floors. Staring back at him from the polished aluminum was an average looking guy. Everyone said he had a jolly face, maybe because it always looked slightly pudgy despite the fact that his five foot nine frame was slim and athletic. But he wasn't jolly. Right now, there was a deep and abiding anger that filled him so full he felt he must burst if he did not release it. How could she do that to him?

The lift hit bottom with a stomach-turning lurch, and the doors slid open. Soon he would be home, and he would have to decide how to cope with the betrayal.

The dark blue Ford looked despondent beneath the sodium lights. Nick climbed in and threw his briefcase onto the back seat. As he turned on the ignition, Bon Jovi screamed of a bullet to the heart and giving love a bad name. The sentiment was perfect, and he turned the car for home and a conversation that had filled his day with dread.

~

Wearing the balaclava was a guilty pleasure. It gave anonymity, but most of all, it gave power. Darkness had fallen over thirty minutes ago, and negotiating the small, neat terrace house was not easy. But eyes adjusted to the dark, and the hunter lived in the shadows, able to lay in wait, able to pounce when needed.

From the front door, there was a narrow hallway and leading off that were two more doors. One to the living room the other to the kitchen. Which would Nick take first? Dressed all in black and clinging to the shadows, the figure paused, left or right? This decision could make all the difference between success and failure. Decision made darkness coalesced around the door on the right and secluded itself into the shadows. Waiting was part hell, part heaven. The anticipation was both thrilling and torturous.

How would he react? Would he fight, or would the first blow knock him to the floor?

Waiting silently, the figure felt the desire, the lust, and a hand reached down to a groin that throbbed with need. The car pulled into the drive. The hunter's breath was fast and shallow, this would not do, he would hear. With a gargantuan effort, it slowed its breathing. Not much longer now.

Nick pulled into the drive and leaned back against his seat. The house was dark, and the driveway empty, so Sadie wasn't home. A mixture of relief and despondency washed over him. At least he had a bit more time to get his mind around their problem, but he still had no idea of what to say. There was no doubt about it, they had married too young. Sadie thought she was pregnant, bloody ironic that was. So he had done the right thing and put a ring on her finger. Three weeks later, the scare was over, and a big part of him had felt cheated. He had wanted children then, had been so looking forward to it, and he desperately wanted them now.

Having just turned thirty-five, Nick felt that time was getting away from him. Sadie was only twenty-eight, but still, if they wanted to enjoy their time with their kids, they needed to get started. She had never told him she didn't want children. In fact, each time they discussed it, she would say, 'If it's meant to be, it will happen.' That was until this morning when he found the packet of pills in her handbag.

Sadie had already left for work, and as often happened, she'd left her purse behind. Working in a chemical lab, she couldn't take much with her and didn't like to leave it in the car. Bile boiled in Nick's stomach as he remembered how he had stood there with the packet in his hand, today's pill was missing. All his hopes, all his dreams seemed to sink from his chest and down to his toes, where they weighed a ton and made it impossible for him to move.

They had supposedly been trying. At times she had joked about liking sex for sex but not as a means to an end. Yet stupidly he had thought they were jokes, why had she never spoken to him about this?

The car ticked as it continued to cool down, and a shiver raised the hairs on Nick's arms. It was time to go in, tonight he had to face the music.

Inside the house behind the kitchen door, the dark figure had not moved it just waited and wondered. What was he doing, why was he waiting? Maybe he was on the phone or just relaxing after a hard day. Well, wasn't he in for a surprise?

Nick walked up to the door, his keys in one hand the briefcase in the other. He would go for a run. That would make him feel better. Pounding the streets would dissipate his anger and give him time to think, maybe he could even work out what to say. The door swung inward, the house was warm but dark. It no longer looked welcoming, but more like a trap. How had he wasted away so many years on someone who did not share his dreams?

As he pushed the front door closed with his foot, the kitchen door moved slightly. Pushed away by the breeze, it stopped when it hit the black figure waiting with anticipation of the pleasures to come.

Nick reached for the light. Flicking it upwards, a grunt of disgust left him when it failed to turn on. *Even the bloody house is against me.*

He shoved the kitchen door with his briefcase. It went harder than he intended and bounced back, smashing into his nose. Pain exploded in his face as the wood struck home. Blood flew out before him, and he reached up stunned as lights seemed to whizz around his head. It felt like something crunched between his fingers, and they came away wet as blood seeped down his face.

What the hell was happening? Had Sadie left something behind the door? Stumbling forward, he felt a whisper of air across the hairs on the back of his neck. *Someone was there.*

Before he could turn, his hands were grabbed, and he was pushed deeper into the kitchen. Fear clasped onto his chest and made the hair on his arms stand to attention. Warm fingers pulled his hands together and shoved them roughly up his back. A grunt escaped him, and his legs rushed forward without his hands to balance him. It felt like he would fall. Panic screamed in his mind, what! Who! Help!

He was grabbed and pulled back and felt something cold and metallic on his hands. As he pulled against his attacker, his wrists were brought together and handcuffed behind him. Terror fought a battle in his chest, and it was winning. The urge to scream and shout, to thrash and kick, was overwhelming, but he was slammed into the wall knocking the breath from his lungs. Kicking backward, he connected with a shin and heard his attacker grunt in pain. Before he could take advantage, he felt a stab to the back of his knees, and he was taken down and then dragged over backward to lie on the cold, hard, tiled floor. In the dark, he did not see the figure as it stepped around him and lowered itself to sit on his chest.

Pain surged through his arms as the weight pushed them to the floor, pulling his shoulders almost out of their sockets and forcing his hands into the small of his back. There was no time for fear, but his chest ached, and his throat was dry, and in the total darkness and without his arms, he had little chance of escaping. Would he die tonight? Would he die without ever becoming a father?

The weight adjusted, moving back towards his groin. Nick rolled his hip and tried to tip his rider onto their head, but they were ready and lifted up. A sharp slap hit his face, and his head rocked sideways and slammed into the hard cold tiles. Momentarily stunned, he sat up and tried to head-butt his attacker. The blow fell woefully short, and he was pushed back, this time accompanied by a subtle giggle.

Once again, the weight shifted. What could he do? The cold hand of fear clasped onto his gut as the weight was settled back down onto his groin. Slowly they worked their hips grinding their seat against his groin in a parody of a lap dance.

"Get off me, you freak," he yelled.

"Really lover, that's the welcome I get."

"Sadie!?"

The shock was complete. Every ounce of energy drained from him, and he let his head fall to the tiles and prayed that this was a dream. His wife would do these strange things. For weeks, she would ignore him, pushing away any advances sexual or otherwise, and then she would seem to explode and would demand sex, often in the most inconvenient of situations. Right now, he was still angry with her, and there was no way that she would use him this way.

"Yes, lover, it's all me. Now, how about a little sugar."

In the dark, Nick felt her fumble with his belt. Deft fingers undid it, and then she was undoing his fly. He gritted his teeth to bite back the anger that threatened to end their marriage.

"No, stop this, damn it, Sadie stop."

With just a slight giggle, she reached in and fondled his dick through his boxers.

This was not gonna happen. He refused to be tied up, beaten, and then fucked in the dark by his bitch of a wife. The bitch who had been lying to him for over a year.

"Get off me damn it, we need to talk." The words were spat at her, and he had trouble holding back the venom that threatened to stream out of him and maybe destroy his marriage forever.

Instead of answering, she slid down his legs, and he felt the soft touch of her lips envelop his flaccid dick. A gasp was wrenched from him, and his hips bucked. Still, she sucked him, rolling him around in the soft wetness of her mouth. Despite himself, Nick felt the familiar heat start deep down in his groin. His cock throbbed in her mouth and rose to the occasion. In his mind, he told himself he would stop this, any minute now, he would tell her about the pills, and he would stop this. The problem was his body had other ideas. He slid in and out of that soft, warm orifice, feeling her lips as they dragged across his cock he could not have stopped it if she had put a gun to his head.

The warmth was building throughout his body, all thought of arguing had gone, and all he could concentrate on was the feeling of her soft lips as they sucked off his dick. Just as he started to feel his orgasm, she pulled away and sat back on his legs. Pain rocked through his shins, but it was not as bad as the loss of her mouth, sucking him, and a groan escaped from his lips.

"Do you want me, lover?" she asked.

"Oh God, yes," he moaned and tried to sit up, but he couldn't, nor could he reach out and touch her.

"Then forgive me my sins," she said, her voice husky and breathless.

Nick knew he had to shout no, and he felt his mouth open to say the word, but all that came out was, "Yes, I forgive you."

The weight lifted off him, and he was filled with loss as his dick throbbed in the cool air, but then she sat back down. Sitting astride him, she took his cock in her hands and guided him into the smooth wetness that was her. She was slick and tight, and he filled her like coming home. Slowly she rose off him until he almost slipped out, and then just as the loss was unbearable, she sat back down and ground her hips against the material of his trousers. He knew he should be mad, but all he could think about was the heat in his dick and the way the sensation rode over him. Taking him up and up like a climb up a roller coaster. He thrilled as he rose to the very pinnacle, and then with a scream, he dropped off the other side. He called out her name as his orgasm slammed into him like a pleasure train filled with nubile ecstasy.

Sadie had never been one to let his orgasm spoil her fun, and she pounded down on him, grinding her pussy into the base of his dick. Then he felt her fingers as she finished herself off. Faster and faster she rubbed across her clit, occasionally her slick fingers would slip into her wetness and brush against his dick, and he started to stir.

It had been a while since he had felt this good, and he let his body respond and ignored the pain in his back and shoulders. His cock throbbed inside her, and a grunt escaped from his lips. Slowly his hips rose, and he pounded into her just as she let out an animal scream of ecstasy as her orgasm pulsed through her. Nick could feel her pussy as it spasmed around his dick. It felt so good that all thoughts of confronting her were gone. All he wanted was to screw her until his brain melted, and all the hurt was forgotten. Sadie dropped forward and rested on his shoulders.

He kissed the top of her head and around onto her forehead, which was covered with something, some silky material cloaked her face. As his hips worked into her, his lips sought out her mouth, they brushed across the material closer. She lifted her head, and Nick sought out her sweet pleasure. Hungry lips slid along her cheek, but then she was gone. She pulled away, and his dick slid out and pointed up at nothing. The cooker light came on, and he saw her stood there all in black, her head covered by a black mask. She peeled it off, and her face was lined with disgust and loathing. She hawked up and spat.

Nick saw her spit and felt the glob hit him just below the eye. "Damn it, Sadie, at least let me loose."

With a toss of her blonde bob, she turned and walked away.

Nick lay back onto the floor. This was not the first time she had behaved like this. It made no sense then, and it made no sense now, but he knew that in an hour or so, she would come around. Treating him as if nothing had happened, she would remove the handcuffs and probably make him a steak and pour him a drink. Until then, he would just have to make himself as comfortable as he could and decide where they went from here.

ick woke on the sofa, his neck stiff, and his throat raw. For a second, he felt good, remembering the orgasm from the previous night a smile spread across his face, but then he tried to move. Cramps ripped through the muscles in his shoulders and down his arm. The battering he had taken from being ridden with his arms behind his back and then being left handcuffed for over an hour would leave residual pain for some time to come. As he woke, he remembered her face as she spat on him when he wanted a second round. She had climbed off and left him there, his hands secured behind him, his trousers down. What the hell was wrong with his psycho of a wife?

Sitting up, the room spun a little, and a wave of nausea swept over him. He remembered banging his head on the tiles and reached back to feel. Sure enough, there was a bump on his skull, he pressed it gingerly and felt the pain spike through him. Leaning forward over his legs, he looked down. "What the?"

Muddy footprints traced across the lounge carpet to where he sat. Looking down, he saw his trainers, neatly tied on his feet. They were coated with mud and had spread the dirt over the side of the sofa as well as the seat cushions. Had he gone for a run last night? It didn't make sense, but this was not the first time he had lost time. What was happening to him?

The house was quiet. Sadie had either gone into work or was still in bed. He could never keep track of her schedule. She worked all hours, and sometimes he found it lonely. The house seemed desolate when she wasn't there. Still, it gave him time to decide how to approach her.

Standing, he found the dizziness had gone, and his legs felt good, his muscles loose. No way had he been for a run, maybe his trainers were muddy from the last time. Maybe he had put them on to empty the bin or something. It didn't matter, he was up, and the morning sunshine splashed through the corner of the blinds and called to him. Things would look better after a run, and if she were here, then they could discuss things over breakfast.

Nick stepped to the fridge and opened the door. He always had an electrolyte drink after his run, and he kept it in a special orange bottle. A smile crossed his face, his bottle was full, sat in the fridge door, and it bore a yellow post-it with a smiley face. Warmth filled him; maybe this was Sadie's way of saying sorry.

With a confident whistle, he was out of the door and set off at an easy jog. The morning sun warmed his back and chased away the problems. Everything always seemed better after a run. It was his alone time, his quiet time, and it allowed his mind to decompress and work out solutions to all of his problems. Well, all except this one, somehow, he thought it would take more than a run to decide what to about Sadie.

Loosening up his stride, he made a quick jog down

the street, and then he turned left and headed into the woodlands. He still didn't feel right. There was a touch of a headache, and he was a little dizzy, a little spaced out like he had drunk too much. It made no sense, but maybe he shouldn't have come out. Maybe he should have had a shower and a few hours more sleep.

Ignoring the doubts, he kicked a little faster. He would run through this, but would he? A few times recently, he had woken not knowing where he was or how he got there. Was he fainting? Sadie just said that he was tired and forgetting that it was nothing to concern him, but now he wondered if that was a lie too.

The track was muddy but solid under his feet, and it was a pleasant run beneath the trees. After about half a mile, his endorphins started to kick in, and both his mind and body began to relax. The tension dropped from his shoulders, and a cloud lifted off his psyche though he still felt weaker than he should do. They could get through this, they could talk things out. Maybe he could work out why she was lying, why she was taking the pill when they both said they wanted children.

Nick turned left again, down a steep muddy track towards the sports field. Then he would run across the field and up the other side before meeting the road and heading back to the house.

As he stepped onto the track, he could see shoe prints. The tread was an Asics Gel track shoe, just like the one he was wearing. Had he run this way yesterday? Or maybe there was another runner who used the same shoe as him? Why was he thinking about running shoes when his marriage was in the sewer? A tree branch caught him across the forehead and brought him back to reality. *Calm yourself.* His breathing was ragged, and so far, he hadn't got his stride. It always took him a while to settle into his run, but once he had, he felt as if he could run forever, and that was when the benefits came, the calmness, the serenity, and the clarity.

The track sloped away from him, and he ducked under another tree branch and turned a corner. On the track was a naked body. A young woman lay, her head toward him, her blonde hair was spread out around her and covered in red-brown smears. Her head was tilted back so that her empty eye sockets stared right at him.

"No, oh God no," Nick screamed and dropped to his knees. Sinking into the mud, he reached out to grab onto something, anything. The world spun, and he felt himself falling, falling, and then there was nothing.

CHAPTER THREE

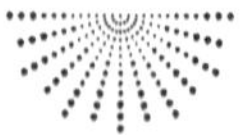

Nick woke to the sun filtering down through the trees. It stung his eyes and gave him a headache as he tried to remember what had happened. Where was he? The realization hit him, he was looking up at the sun flickering through the trees. He had been running. Why did he keep fainting and how come he couldn't remember what had happened. His back was cold and wet, and he reached down. Mud, he was lying on the mud. Slowly he sat up and came face to face with a dead woman.

Empty eye sockets stared back at him, and a scream ripped from his throat. Her face was white, so white, but it looked like her eyes had been ripped from their sockets. Blood lined the empty holes. They were red, raw, and Nick could see gouge marks deep inside the sockets. They filled his vision, holding him with their gaze, forcing him to look into her very soul.

Nick stood and backed away from the accusing eyes. With his mouth open and a greasy feeling in his stomach, he looked back at the woman. Each of her hands was tied to a stake on either side of her head, and her legs were the same, making her a big human X. Blood seeped from around the binding and smeared down her wrists. There were cuts on her body. One beneath each breast and the circular slashes reminded him of a smile. A scream started in his throat, and he had to bite down hard to fight off the hysteria. More wounds were splattered all over her torso. They made deep purple indentations but were clean of blood. Counting quickly, sickly, there were six other wounds, making eight in total. One large wound went from just beneath her breasts all the way down to her blonde curly pubes. Four more surrounded it, and the last was an eight-inch rip across her belly. The skin had been pulled back, and beneath, he could see the viscera and purple intestines bulging, pushing at the gap. They looked like parasites, which wanted to spill out of that hole and come after him. Nick shook his head to clear the thought

Her skin was stark white against the savage wounds. Despite the carnage, she looked so frail, so pure, and so vulnerable. A wave of nausea rose up his gullet, and he turned away, stumbling to his feet and off to the side of the track. Hot bile streamed out of his throat and splashed into the bushes. "Oh my God, oh my God, oh my God." The words kept repeating, and Nick knew he was getting close to panic.

He had to get a grip, to regain control. He should check her pulse. Stumbling forward, he dropped to his knees. The cold mud seeped through his running tights and sucked him down. With a trembling hand, he reached out and touched her wrist. The skin was cold and hard, yet still, he pressed on, his fingers slipping in the blood and smearing it across her wrist. There was no hope, she was hard and cold, but still, he searched. Nothing, there was nothing.

Nick reached up and ran his hand across his face and through his hair. Blood. He looked at his hands, they were covered in blood, and he had just wiped it all across his face. Quickly he rubbed his hands down his clothes and scrubbed off as much of the blood as he could, then he wiped his face with his sleeve.

Something touched his leg, and he jumped back a scream peeling from his throat. *The girl had she grabbed him?*

Nick looked down into the smiling face of a Golden Retriever, and a manic laugh bubbled out of him. It was just a bloody dog. "Hey dog," he said and looked around. Stood on the edge of the trees was a little old woman. She was wearing a long coat and a wooly hat, and her face was frozen in shock.

Nick smiled and then realized that he was covered in either blood or mud, and his hair was probably stuck on end. He was wearing a black running top and tights, so he probably looked to her like some form of ninja assassin, and he had been kneeling over a dead woman. "I err, I just found her," he said as he started to walk toward the woman. "Look, this is not what you think." He pulled out his phone and waved it at her. "Look, I'm gonna call the police. Let them come out here and sort all this out."

"Jinty," the woman shouted. "Jinty, come here." She was backing away from him.

The Goldie gave him a mournful look and trotted off after his mistress.

"Way to go, Nick, cover yourself in the woman's blood and then terrify some old lady." He dialed and waited.

"Emergency, which service, please?"

"Err Police and maybe an ambulance or a morgue wagon or... Damn it, I'm in the woods behind the supermarket, and I've stumbled across a dead woman."

"Officers are on the way, sir. Now I just need to ask a few more questions."

In a daze, Nick confirmed that the girl was dead, even though the operator wanted to talk him through CPR.

"She's dead. Trust me, she's dead," Nick said. Then he guided the police to him as he tried to keep his eyes off the woman lying on the ground.

CHAPTER FOUR

*N*ick folded his arms and leaned back in the cheap plastic chair. Why were these idiots treating him like a suspect?

Detective Inspector Merlin looked across at Police Constable Strike and raised his thick eyebrows. "There's no need to give us attitude, sir. You see, we have a recording of you saying." He paused and made an exaggerated gesture of checking his notes. "She's dead, trust me she's dead. Now, why did you say that?"

Fear replaced the cold, slimy horror that had settled in Nick's gut. It made it hard to think, and he knew that he must pull himself together here. Whatever he told them would stick, so it had better be good. Thoughts of explaining how he had done a first-responders course, came to mind, but all that came out was, "Did you see her?"

"Yes, quite," Merlin said. "Now, if you could just explain one more time what you were doing in the woods."

"Like I told you," Nick said. He stood and waved his hands down his body, emphasizing the running gear and pointing at the dirty trainers. "I was out running. I run that route most days. I came around the corner and saw the..." A wave of nausea came over him, and he had to grab onto his stomach and bite down hard to prevent himself from vomiting all over the interview room. "I saw the body and I... I..." He sat back down, it was impossible to explain to them what had happened. He had been over it so many times, yet they just wouldn't listen.

"Yes, you said you set off from home around seven-thirty in the morning. Yet you didn't call us until five past nine. Looking at the map, you were only half a mile from your home. So, either you're a very slow runner, or you were up to something else before you called us. Now maybe you can see why I'm feeling a little suspicious."

Nick watched as the man licked his thin lips and ran a hand through brown hair cut into a short military style that was receding on both sides of his forehead. Nick could not take his eyes off him. Yet he knew he had to concentrate to bring his mind back to the problem, but he could not focus. Every time he closed his eyes, he saw the bloody empty sockets of the blonde woman, her hair combed out behind her, as those empty eyes accused him.

"I'm waiting for an answer," Merlin said.

Nick scoured his mind. He remembered setting off for a run, his mind full of his own problems, what had happened. Closing his eyes, he imagined the track. He turned the corner and saw the body. A feeling of nausea came over him, and he remembered. "Oh, God, I think I fainted. Look at me. I'm covered in mud. When I woke up, I crawled to the woman, and I checked her pulse. I felt something and looked down, terrified that she was grabbing onto me. It was a dog. Some damn dog was sniffing my legs. There was a woman, an old woman.

I've seen her before, but I'm not sure where she lives. Now come on, you have to believe me that's exactly what happened."

"So you fainted," Merlin said, his eyebrow raised and a look of disdain on his face.

A knock on the door heralded a uniformed PC. He entered the room and walked across to Merlin. They bumped heads and whispered, and the PC handed something to Merlin before leaving. "Well, Mr. Bellamy, can you account for your movements between three and five this morning?"

Nick could feel the man's eyes boring into him, and he wondered did he have an alibi. "I was at home with my wife." God, he just hoped that she would back him up. Having woken on the couch, he wondered if she could even vouch for him, and then there were the muddy trainers. How had he ended up on the couch with filthy trainers? He never left them in that condition, he would always clean them up and leave them in the mudroom, Sadie would go wild if she saw the carpet.

"Do you have a number for your wife, so we can check on your alibi?"

The bottom dropped out of Nick's world, he had no choice, he reached for his mobile and showed them her number.

Detective Inspector Merlin pulled out his own phone, and with a superior look at Nick, he dialed.

Nick held his breath, maybe she wouldn't answer, maybe she would be in the lab, would that be better or worse?

"Mrs. Bellamy, this is Detective Inspector Merlin from Donborough police department. I have your husband with us answering a few questions. I wondered if you could let me know his whereabouts on a couple of occasions... Yes, yes... Now, where was I? Yes, could you tell me if he was with you between three and five this morning?"

Nick watched the other man's face as he listened to his wife. There was no emotion, and he could not read what she was saying. The mood she had been in last night, who knows whether she would help out at all?

"I understand," Merlin said. "Now what about the 23rd of last month between five and nine in the evening... Really... And you have witnesses... Yes, I will be checking into that. Thank you for your time." The DI hung up his phone and pulled his deep brown eyes around and stared directly at Nick.

Nick felt those eyes burning a hole into his head. It felt as if they were boring through him, seeing all of his hopes and fears. With a dry mouth, he tried to ask what was going on, but the words would not come out.

The DI closed his file and stood up.

"Well, Mr. Bellamy, it looks like your alibi checks out for now. We want to thank you for your time and ask you not to leave the area without informing us first. Now you're free to go."

Nick stumbled out of the police station and into the cold, dull day. It suited his mood. They had let him go, but Nick was sure that he was still a suspect. They would be watching him, and if no evidence was found, would he be called in again for questioning. With a resigned sigh, he dialed Sadie. They had to talk. At the very least, he should thank her. As he waited, he wondered if that was the right move. Why should he thank her if he were innocent? The call went through and rang once, twice, and then went to voicemail. Had she just rejected his call? Anger replaced the cold, sick feeling in his gut, and he placed another call, this one to work.

Nick sat in his office and kept his head down, but it appeared he had become quite a celebrity. Rumor had soon spread about his morning, and everyone wanted to come and relive the adventure. Every time he had to speak of the dead girl, acid boiled in his stomach and threatened to rush up his throat and redecorate his desk. The afternoon dragged. Eventually, he stuck a sign outside, 'Busy Need Quiet,' and closed his door. That stopped the steady stream of verbal looky-loos and allowed him to still his mind by concentrating on the quarter's accounts.

The office was quiet, and Nick looked up. Everyone had gone home, the lights were off, and the building looked empty, a check of his watch told him it was seven and he was late. How had he become so involved? Never mind he should rush home, Sadie would be waiting, and the last thing he needed to do was get her angry... again.

Nick stood and felt dizzy. Slumping back into his chair, he took big deep breaths and then tried again. The room wobbled but not as bad as last time. What was wrong with him? Earlier, he had fainted, he had no idea how he got to sleep on the couch, or why he was wearing his trainers, and now he was finding it hard to stand up. A groan from his stomach reminded him that he had not eaten today. Well, that accounted for today, of course seeing a dead... brutally murdered body accounted for this morning. But if he was honest, he had been losing time for a couple of weeks now. His run had become more difficult, and he often got stomach pains and headaches. Maybe he should get a checkup?

Somehow he got into the car and drove the Ford home all the time wondering how Sadie would be and what she would say about this morning. Come to think of it what had happened last night?

The lights were on, but the warming glow filled him with dread, and he sat in the car a moment longer, building up the courage to enter. There had been a time when coming home was filled with joy, now it was often faced with a sense of trepidation. Opening the car door, he attempted to stand, but his knees gave way, and a wave of nausea flowed over him.

Sitting back down, he closed his eyes and relaxed. He would just take a moment, then he would be able to go inside, and he had to talk to Sadie about something, something important. The problem was, he couldn't remember what it was.

CHAPTER FIVE

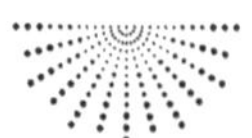

Nick woke, his neck stiff, his body cold, and his stomach churned with both hunger and a greasy sickness that threatened to flood his throat with bile. What was he doing sleeping in his car? Had he fallen out with Sadie? It was possible, they had something to discuss, had they talked about it? What was it? The problem was, no matter how much he tried, he couldn't remember. It was important, and it mattered to him, yet he couldn't remember if they had talked about it. If there had been a fight surely, he would have a memory of that.

The house still glowed with warm, welcoming light, yet when he thought about going in, his stomach heaved and threatened to erupt. *What time was it?* A quick look at his watch told him it was nine. What had he been doing? He left the office around seven; it was a twenty-minute ride home. That meant he had been asleep in his car for over an hour and a half. What on earth was going on?

Nick opened the door and swung his legs out. Slowly he tested with his weight, they held, and he felt fine. Now he had to face the music. The door was locked, so he found his key and entered. The hallway was dark, but he could hear the television. Trepidation stroked down his spine as he pushed open the door to the lounge.

The lighting was muted, the television was playing twenty-four-hour news, and an image of the wood almost dropped him to his knees. Sadie lay on the sofa, wearing a short, flimsy negligee. Her face wore a salacious grin as she beckoned him forward.

Nick moved to the easy chair opposite her and slumped down.

"Well, lover, you up for some fun?" she asked.

Nick could not peel his eyes off the television. The girl was a Jane Doe and the thought that nobody knew she was missing, that nobody missed her filled him with a cold sadness that shrank his heart and withered his spine. They put up a composite of her face and asked for anyone who knew her to get in contact. Nick felt tears coursing down his face. She was only twenty-two years old. So young to be dead.

"Hey, babe, are you alright?" Sadie asked as she crossed the room.

Nick wanted her dressed, wanted her to keep her distance, wanted to shout and scream at her that no, he wasn't alright, but instead, he just shrugged.

Like a cat, she rose and stalked over to him. Sitting on the arm of the chair. He could feel the warmth of her skin through his trousers. An arm came around his shoulder, and she pulled him to her.

"What happened today?" she asked, she sounded genuinely concerned.

Tears flooded out of Nick's eyes, dribbled down his face and fell into his lap. The words came after. How he'd woken on the sofa, how he went for his run and how he had found a poor young girl brutally murdered and tied down in the dirt. He was blubbing as he told her of Detective Inspector

Merlin and having to ask for an alibi. She hugged him close and rocked him while he cried, and slowly, the pain diminished, and life came back into focus.

"Why didn't you answer my call?" he asked.

"When Sweetie?"

"After I left the police station, I don't know what time it was. I needed to talk, and you rejected my call damn it."

A silky laugh left her throat and stroked his taut nerves. "I went straight into the lab. I'm sorry, Sweetie, that police chappy only just caught me. You know my work and how time-sensitive it can be."

Nick nodded, but the problem was he didn't. She worked with chemicals, and it was all very secretive. If she ever did explain anything, it went straight over his head, all those numbers and letters, nothing had a name. There was nothing for him to clasp onto, and at times he thought she made it more complicated just to belittle him. Now he was getting paranoid!

She stroked his head, and it was nice to lie in her arms and feel her breathing. It was relaxing, comforting. Exhaustion overcame him, and he felt himself slip down into a deep sleep.

He dreamt of the girl and an eight-inch serrated hunting knife that Sadie had given him last Christmas. It had been a strange gift. At the time, he had tried to hide his disappointment but had failed miserably. They ended up rowing about it. She had sulked for two days and then, as usual, she had come to him, apologetic and loving.

"You asked for it," she said. "Don't you remember?"

The thing was he didn't. In fact, he couldn't imagine a situation when he would want a hunting knife. His only hobby was his running, surely she knew that.

In the dream, this all chased through his mind, but then he picked up the knife, and he felt a surge of power. It was sexual in its intensity, he reached down and adjusted his dick. In his dream, he closed his eyes and thrilled at the feeling of dominance the knife gave him. It pulsed through his body, euphoric in its intensity.

Opening his eyes, he was on a side street. It was dark, and the streetlight above him flickered on and off like some convulsive disco light. Where was he?

Gradually his senses kicked in. It was the other side of the woods, a rough area, maybe he shouldn't be here. Then he felt the knife in his hands and confidence surged through him. He had nothing to fear. He was the one to fear.

A car pulled up, a rusty old Vauxhall, and a young girl got out. Her blonde bob hung tiredly around her shoulders as she stumbled over to her door. Wobbling a little, she fumbled with her keys. Where had he seen her before?

Panic rushed into him along with a dirty, naughty thrill. He was hunting. Silently he crossed the roads as the blonde dropped her keys, unaware that death stalked towards her like a whisper on the wind.

Bending down, he could see her long legs beneath the coat. They were shapely and fit, and the urge to run his hands up them and feel the sweet treasure that waited at their top made him stumble down the curb. "Shit," he cursed under his breath, but she had seen him.

Turning, her eyes were so wide they lit up her face and beckoned him onward. Dropping into a squat, she searched for the keys, desperate now that she had seen the hunter and realized that she was the prey. Scraping her hand along the ground, he could hear whimpers of fear that sounded almost like she was close to her orgasm. Soon my pretty he thought. There was no longer any need to stalk. She knew he was here. Now it was simply a matter of who was faster. The hunter or the hunted.

In his mind, Nick felt a wave of revulsion, *stop, what are you doing?* Then it was gone, and his body took over. His feet flew across the tarmac, the knife gliding forward in his left hand as he pumped his arms to gain every second of speed he could. In his right there was a cloth, it smelt funny and he couldn't remember how it got there. *Maybe Sadie left it out.* It gave off a chemical smell. That was not unusual, she was always bringing jars and tubes of unpronounceable things home.

The girl found her keys and stood. Now the sound coming from her throat was a high pitched keen, over and over again. It was as if she was trying to scream, but her throat was closed down so tight it could only manage this siren call of sorrow and despair.

She turned the keys over in her hands, glancing at him, then back to the bundle. At last, she found the right one and touched metal to metal. Safety was so close he could smell it coming off her in big waves of relief. Nick leaped the last step, and his left hand-delivered the knife into her kidneys. It tore through her coat and clothes without even slowing. There was a slight hesitation as it hit her skin. Pushed forward by his weight and speed, Nick felt the knife as it sliced through skin, muscle, organ, and then it bounced back at him as it hit bone. He thrust into her and let out an orgasmic grunt of pleasure. At the same time, his right hand came up and covered her mouth and nose. It stifled the scream that had at last formed on her lips, and he pulled the cloth harder. Instinct told him that the chemical would silence her, and give him more time.

As he thrust into her, she pushed back, wanting more, he thought, and he gave it to her. The blade pulled out, its edge serrated for extra pleasure, it caught, but he pulled it free. Her juices flowed over his hands, and with a feeling of rapture, he plunged back in, taking her to the pinnacles of... death?

What am I doing?

Like a trapped bird, she fought in his arms. Her tiny wings pushed back, but they had no strength, no power, and she was fading. Whether from the pleasure from their encounter or the cloth over her face, he could not tell. Letting his right hand drop to his side, he wanted to step back, to wake up, and then, he heard Sadie's voice.

"Give it to her baby."

It was as if some animal took over. His arm plunged forward, and the knife went back in, he pulled out and thrust in, again and again, grunting with pleasure and effort as he rose to new heights of ecstasy. All the time, he rubbed his dick against her legs, and the slick feeling of her blood brought him higher until with a final thrust, he came and collapsed forward. Stepping back, he turned her around, wanting to see her face, to kiss her. Wide, terrified eyes had closed, her face was relaxed and tender after their loving. He licked the sweat from her top lip and kissed her. She tasted salty and young and slightly of rice pudding. Nick pulled back, he was not finished, as he did her eyes came open, it was no longer the blonde. It was Sadie in his arms, she opened her mouth and holding the knife she said, "Would you die for me, darling?"

Before he could nod a yes, she plunged the knife into him.

Pain and revulsion jerked him awake. His eyes shot open and looked straight into Sadie's big blue ones. Wearing a neutral expression, she was leaning over him. Looking at him as if he were some experiment that she evaluating. It was too much. Nick shot off the sofa and ran to the bathroom, too late. He fell to his knees and sank to the carpet, and a long, caustic stream of vomit burned its way out of him and sank into the rug.

CHAPTER SIX

It had been a long night. Nick spent most of it lying in their bed. The soft duvet provided warmth and security as he cried in Sadie's arms. The problem was he wasn't sure why he cried. The dream had been horrific, nauseating, and yet exciting. It was just a dream... a fantasy? Had he killed that girl? Turning it over in his mind and feeling sick to his stomach, he fell back to sleep. This time the dream was not so nice. He was stalked. Hunted by the darkness of his conscience. There was nowhere to hide, and the fear that he was a killer brought terror to his heart.

When he woke, Sadie was gone, the bed cold and desolate. As he remembered the night before, bile rose up his throat and threatened to spill all over the white sheets. Biting it back, he dressed and showered. Somehow he felt better today, more alert and less dizzy. Maybe he was coming down with something, and that was why he kept losing time. Maybe he should book into the doctors and get a checkup. *Yeah, just don't mention the vivid dreams about killing a girl, oh yeah, and the fact that she's dead.*

As he came down the stairs, his hand on the rail, the soft green carpet beneath his feet, he could hear whistling. "At least you woke up happy?" he said as he stepped into the kitchen.

The room was always immaculate; Sadie kept it like her lab. Everything was sterile, and everything was in its place.

"A good morning to you too," she said, and with a quick peck on his cheek, she popped a plate of toast on the table and passed him the jam. "Are you going for a run this morning? I already mixed up your special drink."

Nick's stomach roiled and gurgled at the smell of the toast. He was hungry, even felt a little weak, but the thought of eating right now just made him want to wretch again. Should he go for a run, get some clarity before they had their talk? Maybe he should leave the talk for another day? The problem was it would eat away at him, and that was probably why he was feeling so ill. The distrust he felt, the betrayal, stayed in his head, he did not want to give her time to think or to make up some excuse and duck out on him. "No, not this morning. Eat your breakfast. We need to talk."

"Okay, sweetie, mine's in the oven ready." With that, she pulled out a plate of egg, bacon, mushrooms, and sausage.

It looked and smelled scrumptious, but his stomach heaved, and he had to run from the room. Nick slammed through the toilet door and dropped to his knees on the hard tiles just in time to wretch into the bowl. His stomach was empty, so all that came out was a dribble of acid. Still, his stomach heaved again and again. At last, it stopped, and he rested his head on the porcelain, his abs ached, and his stomach just felt slick and greasy.

Back at the table, let's try again, he took a mouthful

of coffee and tried to nibble on his toast. It was cold and dry and clogged in his throat.

Sadie pushed away her plate and ran a hand through her hair. It struck Nick like a lightning bolt, the dead woman, she looked like Sadie. It had to be a coincident, and the resemblance was only slight. Yeah, his inner voice said the same hair, the same height, and the same weight. Her face was not quite the same; Sadie had an oval face that made her look young and innocent. "Oh God," he groaned.

"What's wrong?" she asked.

"The girl who died, I think she looked like you." The enormity of it was like a punch to the gut.

"Really. That's just what every wife wants to hear, you look like a corpse. Was she as attractive?"

Attractive. "I don't really know, she was dead, her eyes ripped from her face it was awful."

She looked down at her food and pushed the nearly empty plate away. "I think we should talk about something else. Something, anything, to try and take your mind off this."

"Okay," he said. He wanted to confront her to shout

and scream and call her a bitch, but somehow, this still didn't seem like the right time. There were tears forming in her eyes, he could see the telltale signs, the quiver of her lip, and the moisture behind her lashes. It had always crushed him to see her cry, but just for a moment, he wondered if this was another manipulation. Then he shook his head, he really was getting paranoid. "Any ideas?" he asked.

"I have to tell you something." She was looking straight at him.

He had seen this look before too, she was trying to be confident, but she knew he would hate what she had to say. "Okay," he said, but there was a lump in his throat and the cold hand of fear in his gut. Was she sleeping with someone?

"I've had a promotion at work. Because of that, I've had to rethink my plans..."

She let the words hang, and all he could think of was she's leaving me, how can she be leaving me?

"Nick, I can't have children... not just now... I've been meaning to tell you, wanting to tell you, but I knew how hurt you would be, and so instead, I went back on the pill, and now I feel like such a bitch."

"What?" Nick heard the words, and it was as simple as that, she had changed her mind. Her damn career was more important than they were, and she didn't even tell him first.

"Look, I'm sorry," she said and got up and walked around to him.

A gentle hand touched his shoulder, and he wanted to push it off to jump up and ram her into the wall. In fact, right then, he wanted to bang her head on the table, pull down her jeans, and fuck her over the breakfast pots. Instead, he bit down his anger. "You couldn't discuss this with me first?" There was acid in his tone, and she stepped away.

"This is important to me," she said. "It's more money, more responsibility. I may even get to design new chemicals. This could be groundbreaking."

"You know how much I wanted a child?" This time his voice sounded petulant. "Is it so much to ask that we do what most couples do and have children? Damn it, Sadie, I would do anything for you."

"I know you would, and we will have children, but just not now..." Her words trailed off as she realized just how disgusted he was. "Remember what we used to say what I used to ask you?"

This time there was a lightness to her voice as if she was teasing, and he was not in the mood. Of course, he remembered. It had always seemed a little creepy, even when they were in the throes of young love. There was no way he would say the words.

He had been looking down at his hands on the table, at the remains of the dry toast when her laugh went through him like a knife to the bone.

"I used to ask you. Would you die for me, darling, and you would reply, of course, I would." Her face was smug as if she had beaten him. "I'm not asking for you to die for me, all I'm asking is for a little more time, to let me get this job under my belt before I go off on maternity leave. All right, Sweetie."

Nick felt like a shit. When she put it like that, it made him sound like a real dick. Some jerk who wanted her to give up her dream just so he could have kids, but he thought it was her dream too. "I understand," he said, but the words were hard to say, and they seemed to clog his throat. "I just need to know how long we have to wait."

Her laughter was like water on a tin roof. It jarred his nerves and irritated. "Just a year, at the most two. You can do that for me, can't you, darling?"

Nick nodded and wondered how many years this would turn into, maybe he should think about leaving.

"That's so good of you, and I will make it up to you, but now I have to run I have an MMA demo in forty minutes, bye." With that, she turned, grabbed her kit bag, and walked out.

When she was gone, the house was so quiet. Nick sat and wondered why he had stopped the Mixed Martial Arts they both used to enjoy. This time it was him that laughed. He had stopped because she was a natural. She was soon competing and winning while he could hardly master the basic kicks. She had a determination and animal-like skill that meant few could beat her when she put her mind to it. Now she competed at the national level, and she was good. That's just what he needed, not only did she not want kids, but she could whoop his ass anytime she wanted.

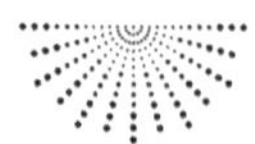

Nick decided to go for his run, but today he opted for the streets. Somehow the woods were too scary, and he did not think he would be able to relax. Every corner would hide unimaginable horrors. Even now, if he closed his eyes, he could see the girl's empty sockets rimmed with blood.

Thinking about his dream, he tripped off a curb and almost went down. Get a grip, man. Why was he so tired? Why was the run not renewing him like it usually did? Of course, he had still done nothing about that doctor's appointment. It was too late today he would book in first thing Monday.

The run back was just as bad, He tripped, lost his breath even got a stitch at one point. It had been a disaster, and he felt weak and dizzy instead of alert and energized. Taking off his trainers, he left them neat in the mudroom and stumbled into the kitchen. Grabbing his energy drink from the fridge, he would usually rush up and shower. It always left him invigorated after a run but not this week. This week he just felt tired. Slumping onto the sofa, he switched on the TV and relaxed back. Closing his eyes, he took a drink and reveled in the buzz the energy drink gave him. Yet still, he felt tired. It must be all the stress, he would just close his eyes, just have five minutes, and then he would shower.

The sound of the door slamming woke Nick. He jerked upright, it was dark outside, what the... Had he been asleep all day? A groan from his stomach was accompanied by the sound of Sadie putting away her equipment. The routine was always the same. Put down her bag, pull out her soiled clothes, and put them straight in the washer. Then place her bag in the cupboard.

Once everything was tidy, she would switch on the kettle and then come look for him. Shit – he was still in his running gear, and he was lying on the sofa. His neat-freak of a wife would have a dickey fit.

Nick raced up the stairs and jumped in the shower. As he stood under the streaming water, his heart pounded, and he felt faint.

The rest of the evening was spent in their normal routine. They watched TV, they talked, Sadie practiced some of her routines, she even offered to spar with him, but Nick didn't have the energy to be humiliated again. Around eleven, they went up to bed. He climbed under the covers and wondered whether to make a move. It all seemed so surreal. She turned toward him and reached over and kissed his forehead. Then she stroked his eyes closed and kissed each of his eyelids, and that was the last thing he remembered.

Nick woke to the sound of ringing. Pulling the covers over his head, he snuggled back down, but the noise just wouldn't go away. His head ached, and at last, he realized that it was the phone. Opening his eyes, he reached across and picked it up. "Hello."

"Nick, where are you?" John seemed to yell down the phone.

"What... What time is it?"

"Eleven thirty, and you missed the board meeting. Luckily ole John here covered for you. I wondered if you had to go see the police again," John said.

"What?"

Ah, came down the phone. "I can see you're in top form this morning. Have you seen the news?"

Nick cleared his throat and ran a hand through his hair, concentrate. "No, what news?" Three whole words, he was waking up.

"That Gillian from the account you were working last year. She was found murdered this morning. The news said it was brutal. I told the boss you had a doctor's appointment, so shake a leg and get in here pronto."

Nick put down the phone and raced to the bathroom. Hot vomit streamed out of him, splashing on the toilet seat before he could get fully over the bowl. Sinking to his knees, he tried to remember Gillian, and a smile of relief came over his face. She was fat, well plump, and she had long ginger hair. She looked nothing like Sadie. The sense of relief was overwhelming, and it kept him smiling until he walked back into the bedroom and saw his trainers next to the bed. There was mud on the carpet, how had Sadie not noticed?

Nick stumbled into work after having the good sense to book a doctor's appointment for Friday at nine in the morning. Taking the time to thank John, he got his head down and tried to concentrate on the job at hand. Yet every few minutes, he was thinking about the muddy footprints on the bedroom carpet and the trainers next to the bed. The thought that he might have killed these girls left him in a cold sweat, and once again, he had been unable to eat anything this morning.

When the tea trolley came round, he grabbed a coffee and a muffin and retired back into his office. So far, he had done nothing, just shifted paperwork, and stared at figures. What was wrong with him?

Then a thought sent a spike of pain through his skull and seemed to squeeze his heart until it would pop. His pulse was racing, and sweat had broken out on his forehead and back. What if he was a schizophrenic, what if he was killing these girls and just didn't remember?

Flicking onto Google, he did a quick search. Some of the symptoms matched muddled thinking, loss of memory, but that was all. It gave no reason for him to be killing girls, and then it hit him, multiple personality disorders. Did he have a split personality? Quickly he typed in the search for the symptoms of this disorder, and just as he pressed enter, there was a knock on the door.

"Come in," he said quickly, flicking over to another window.

"Hello, Mr. Bellamy. If you remember, I'm Detective Inspector Merlin, and I would like you to come down to the station to discuss a few things with us."

Nick's breath froze in his throat, his chest ached with the pounding his heart was giving it, and he doubted if he could stand even if they forced him. Clearing his throat gave him time to think. "Is that a request? Because if so, maybe I could come later, after work?"

"Yes, it is a request, but I would prefer it if you came now. A young lady is dead, after all."

"I know nothing about that," Nick said and knew it sounded pathetic.

"Still, sir, if you don't mind."

ick sat in the interrogation room, wondering if he needed a lawyer. So far, all they had done was ask him about his movements over and over again.

"Like I said," Nick repeated. "I overslept. I've been feeling unwell. In fact, I think I'm coming down with something, and I'm going to the doctor."

"So, no one knows where you were at midnight then?" Merlin asked.

"I was in bed with my wife. Why don't you ring her?"

Merlin put on a smug expression. "Well, sir, we

already have. She remembers taking a sleeping pill, she also thinks you got up in the night, but she can't remember the time."

Bitch, went through Nick's head. "She never takes a sleeping pill, she doesn't believe in them." A vision of the muddy footprints on the beige bedroom carpet came into his mind, but he shrugged them away, no way had he killed a girl in his sleep.

Merlin opened a file and pulled out a photo. It was a pretty girl, blonde hair cut into a shoulder-length bob. She had a pretty oval face, and she looked so like his wife that his face dropped. His mouth sprung open, and he felt the color drain from his face. What was happening?

"I see you know her," Merlin said.

"No... No, I don't." And he didn't, but as he looked closer, the set of the eyes, the mouth, was this Gillian Jones?

"So you do know her," Merlin pressed. "You may as well admit it, Mr. Bellamy, because we have your company's records.

"I... she could be a girl I dealt with a few years ago,

but she's so much slimmer, and her hair is a different color. I'm just not sure. Is she dead?"

"What would you know about that?" Merlin asked.

Nick tried to ignore the slimy grin on the man's face. They thought they had him, but no way had he killed her. Yet as he opened his mouth to talk, a nagging doubt picked at his brain. Pick, pick, pick – had he killed her? "I... I... Look, you've brought me in here... I have to assume you're showing me her picture because something happened."

Merlin slid the picture back into his file and pulled out another one. In this, the girl was transformed. Empty eyes, red, raw, and butchered stared back at him. They held his gaze, accusing, pointing at him, and almost demanding his head. The picture was like a punch to the gut, and Nick felt his stomach turn. He jumped up from the table. Bile rose up his throat and into his mouth. Biting down he scanned the room, there was a bin in the corner, he leaped from the chair and raced to the bin. Just in time for vomit to stream out of him in one long caustic gag reflex.

"Sit back down, Mr. Bellamy," Merlin shouted.

Nick dropped to his knees, and dry heaved into the plastic. At last, the spasms stopped leaving his throat raw, his abs aching and a slick bitter taste in his mouth. Spitting out the last dregs and trying to rid his mouth of trails of saliva, he sat back on his heels. "Are you kidding me?"

"Sit down and look at the picture," Merlin's voice demanded.

As if in a trance, Nick did as he was told. Seeing the picture caused another convulsion in his gut, but he held back and tried to look. "I didn't do this," he said. "Why would I do this?"

Merlin placed the file over the picture and stared into Nick's eyes. The seconds ticked past, and Nick felt as if his very soul was being observed. It took all his control to keep his face calm, neutral, and at last, the man broke his gaze.

"In that case," Merlin said. "I would like you to write down your account of this morning. When you woke, who you spoke to, how you got here. Can you do that?"

Nick nodded and took the paper and pen offered. With a shaky hand, he did as he was bid while the smug bastard sat watching him; his arms folded his eyes blank. Finished, he handed the paperback and watched as Merlin took it from him, stood up, and left the room.

As the door closed, Nick felt a mixture of fear and relief. It was good to be out of the cop's gaze, but he had to wonder what he had just done. Trying to relax, he closed his eyes, but fatigue overtook him, and he had to stand and slap his face to stay awake. This was ridiculous, his freedom was in danger, people were dying, and yet he needed to sleep.

Outside the interview room, Merlin met a tall, bald man with a kind face. Shaun was their handwriting expert, and with excitement in his gut, he handed over the paper. "How long to analyze this?" he asked.

"Not long."

They walked together down the faded gray corridor and into Shaun's office. It was cluttered with paper and files, and Merlin wondered how he ever managed to find anything. There was a bench at chest height on one wall. It sloped away from them, and Shaun placed the paper on its surface. To one side was a twelve by ten photo of a naked back. Carved into the skin was a heart. The edges of the wound had bled down, and to Merlin, it looked as if the skin had cried blood. He shook his head. This was no time to be feeling sentimental. Next to the photo was a small note about A6 in size. It was sealed in an evidence bag, and next to it was an enlargement of the note.

Shaun pulled an overhead light, on an extendable arm, down to shine on the table. To Merlin, it bounced off the white surface and seared into his eyes. He closed them for a second; this was no time to give in to fatigue. This bastard had killed twice, and there was no sign of him stopping unless Merlin could find the evidence.

Opening his eyes, he watched as Shaun leaned over the writing, his head nodded slightly as he moved over each word. Then he looked to the left, checking the evidence bag. Merlin moved in closer and peered over his back. He could see Nick's writing on the right. It looked the same to him as the writing on the left, the writing that had chilled his blood this morning. A note had been found under both bodies. They read, 'Would you die for me, darling?'

Shaun stood upright and turned around so quickly that the two men were toe to toe, and Merlin jumped back. "Well?" he asked, recovering some composure.

Shaun nodded. "They are similar, and there are matching points. However."

Merlin heard the word, and his world dropped out from beneath him, this was the last thing he needed to hear.

Shaun had paused as he saw the detective's face, but he continued. "However, they are not a match."

"Is that it?" Merlin asked. "Can't you give me any more? Maybe he could have altered his writing, made it look less like his?"

Shaun shook his head. "That's not possible. Even if you change your writing, there are base points that look the same. You slip them in subconsciously, and that is what we look for. This is a small sample." He tapped the evidence bag. "So my findings are not one hundred percent, but in all honesty, I don't believe these were written by the same man."

"You have to give me something?" Merlin said, knowing that he sounded desperate.

This time Shaun dropped his head and seemed to wait. At last, he looked up. "It will have to be off the record."

Merlin nodded; there was an understanding between them.

"Alright," Shaun said. "Off the record, I would say that this looks like someone trying to forge his handwriting."

"You're telling me someone is trying to frame him?"

"Maybe," Shaun said. "The only other possibility is split personalities, but remember, this is not an exact science, it's my opinion. I could be wrong."

Merlin left the office with a sinking feeling in his gut, and fatigue seemed to crush him. This had been a total waste of time, he had nothing, and he had to let Nick go. How many more women would die screaming before he could catch this bastard?

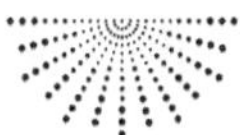

CHAPTER NINE

Sara stepped off the bus and into the cold night. Pulling her coat around her ears, she regretted staying at work so late, almost as much as she regretted catching the last bus and not opting for a taxi. Still, it was only a short walk home, and the street lights made it feel safer.

There was no traffic, and she crossed the road and lengthened her stride glad she had worn trousers today and that her heels weren't too high. All she had to do was walk along Sycamore, cross over Oak, and she would be back on Basil. Her mind was half on the drawing she had completed today. It was good work, probably her best, and she was proud of it. Heat warmed her cheeks as she thought of the client, he was lush, and she had put in some extra hours to make sure he was impressed. Tomorrow they were meeting for lunch to discuss the project, so she needed to get home and sleep. She was looking for more than professional courtesy, and it was more than her drawings she wanted him to find impressive.

Up ahead was a ginnel, it would take a few minutes off her journey, and she had done it many times before. Yes, she would take it, but as she approached the unlit cut through, it looked dark and unwelcoming, anyone could be hiding within the shadows. Admonishing her cowardice, she still ignored the shorter route and continued on under the street lights. After all, two women had been murdered in the town recently, why didn't she take that taxi?

Pulling her mind back to safer ground, she wondered what she should wear tomorrow. This had been going through her mind all week. Every time she heard his silky voice and thought about the deep blue of his eyes and the sun-kissed hair, she had wondered and worried. She was sure he was interested, and all he needed was a little extra push. Still, she had to look professional, but still, she wanted something just a little enticing. It came to her, she had a figure-hugging black shift dress. It was totally right and cut just a little lower than she normally found comfortable. If she wore a black jacket, she could take it off as the luncheon warmed up a little.

She was nearly home and feeling satisfied when she spotted a shadow. As she walked past a house, something reflected in the window. It was dark and moved behind her, but as she turned her head to look, it was gone. She stared back at herself in the black pane of glass, and behind her, the street was deserted. There was just a car and someone's dustbin, but nothing moved.

Quickening her pace, she set off again, but now there was a catch in her breath, and her heart pounded against her chest. It was nothing, just a shadow. So why did she feel like a rabbit? In her mind, the fox took its time, waiting in the bushes for just the right moment to pounce.

"Stop this," she whispered, but the hairs had risen on her arms, and fear fluttered like a trapped bird in her stomach.

She turned onto Basil and could see her front gate. It

was so close, she was home, and these foolish feelings would look just like that once she was safe within its walls.

A noise behind caused her to jump inside. It sounded like a foot scuffing the concrete. Hurrying towards the gate, she glanced back. There was a shadow on the wall. Someone was following her. No, more than that, they were hiding. They didn't want her to know.

She set off at a run and sprinted the last few paces to her gate. Footsteps pursued her. No longer cautious, whoever was behind, closed the gap. Sara wanted to look back, but she knew if she did, it would slow her progress. Reaching the gate, her hand clasped onto the cold metal, and she reached down for the clasp. It was always tricky and once again regret clouded her mind, why hadn't she got it fixed. She pushed but missed the catch and rammed into the gate. It scraped against her thighs, and panic filled her, making her hand slip on the cold iron, but this time she had it, and the gate swung inward.

Reaching in her pocket, she fumbled for the keys. Finding them, she pulled them out just as she heard the gate move. Her pursuer was close. The keys jangled in her hands as she searched for the right one. Yes, she had it, and it slid home and turned. She was safe.

Sara pushed the door and stepped in just as she was punched in the back. It stung, and she cursed but kept going just as a hand reached around her. Something that smelt sickly and sweet was placed over her mouth.

Panic like a vicious beast clawed at her, and she thrashed her arms clawed for the hand at her mouth. Deep inside, a voice told her to remember her self-defense training. To reach down and go for the balls but her hands would not obey, and she clawed at the thing that clamped over her mouth. DNA, scratch him, she thought, but it was leather that her nails dug into, and she was fading. It would be fine to rest for just a little while. Her hands dropped to her side, and luckily, she was caught as she collapsed against her attacker.

The figure pulled her inside and kicked the door closed. The light was not needed, the house would be better in darkness. Lifting the girl, it stepped into the house and through to the kitchen. Perfect. Drawing the blind, a hand was swept across the worktop, sweeping pots and a sugar bowl to one side. The girl was laid face down.

Blood oozed from her back, but the knife had missed her kidney, and the flow was clean and steady. There was a little time yet. From within a pocket, an eight-inch long serrated hunting knife was produced, and in the semi-light, it sliced easily through the girl's thick coat and her thin blouse.

Breathing heavily, the figure smiled as the knife slid across smooth skin. This was the best bit, this was the enjoyment. Observing the sharp knife as it shaved skin before sinking into a living, breathing human and then watching as the lifeblood flowed out. It was euphoric, it was God-like.

CHAPTER TEN

Time was short. As a hunter, the night was a friend and dawn an enemy, and yet the sun was coming, and there was nothing that could be done to stop it.

The girl had been rolled over onto her back, stripped naked and strapped to the work surface. It was an ingenious design. Packing straps held the body tight and were secured with a small nail gun. The countertop would never be the same again, but that was someone else's problem. Everything was portable and easy to carry, and every care was made that DNA, hair, and fingerprints were not left at the scene. Still, the hunter was confident that they would not be caught. Planning was key, as was the preparation. The girl had been watched for weeks, and everything was in place. The transformation would take about an hour, and then she would be left for viewing. For everyone to see what a hooker she was and they would know, she deserved everything that she got.

Eyes closed, blonde shoulder-length hair combed out behind her, she looked almost serene. She had nice boobs, firm but large and a fit, attractive body. Tan lines marked her arms and legs, and there was a scar across her stomach. It was interesting, and a good place to start, no, maybe to finish. Still, she breathed easily and slowly, and there was no sign that she would wake.

This was the trickiest part, waiting for her to come around. Waiting and wondering if the dosage was too much and she would sleep on, not waking in time for the party. The most important one of her life, the one she really did not want to miss.

Standing back, breath coming faster and faster with the anticipation of the fun to come was part torture, part pleasure. A hand reached across a chest tensed and expectant and then down to a groin that throbbed with desire.

Excitement caused a gasp of air, she was waking. Her eyes fluttered open and then closed. So far, she thought this was normal, did not realize what was about to begin. Quickly, before she started to scream, from a bag on the floor, a ball-gag was produced and pushed into her mouth then fastened behind her head. The rough handling brought her fully conscious and frightened eyes widened as she realized the predicament she was in. In the dim light, she could not see too well. But she would feel the cold counter beneath her back, feel the straps across her naked body, and feel the cuts in her skin as they opened as she strained against her restraints. It was always the same, they tried to scream, tried to fight. Their bodies convulsed as they struggled against their ties.

It was best to stand quietly and enjoy the show. Sooner or later, she would exhaust herself and quiet down. Then it would be time to start. Sometimes, when they saw death stood before them, their bladder would empty, and the sharp smell of urine would fill the room, but not tonight. It looked like Sara had control.

She stopped, lay still, and it was as if she willed her eyes to penetrate the dark and search out the danger. Good, it was time to start.

Sara fought against the straps that held her with everything she had. A cold, hard panic had settled in her stomach and momentarily frozen her limbs, but that would not get her out of this. She was a fighter, and she would fight. Where was she? As the question entered her mind, so did the answer. It was her kitchen; she could feel the tiled work surface, the one she always intended to change. That meant she was still at home. It was hard to stay calm when you were strapped naked to the counter, not knowing why or by who, but she must. If she was to survive this, she must think.

As she thrashed with all her might, four straps dug into her skin. One across her ankles prevented her from moving her feet from side to side, but maybe she could bend her leg and pull backward.

The second strap was across her thighs, and it held her legs down so hard that she did not have enough movement to move her lower legs and free her feet.

The third strap held her hips down tight, and the fourth was above her breasts. Harder, she struggled as panic took full control. She bucked and convulsed her body, tried to shake her arms, and pound her legs, but the only thing moving was her head and neck, and that just caused her pain. At last, exhaustion made her lie still, and that was when she noticed the pain in her back. It felt like she had been sliced open, and salt had been rubbed into the wounds.

Controlling her breathing, controlling her panic, she tried to keep still, to adjust to the dark, and to work out who would do this to her. No one came to mind. A light came on, subdued but stark. Someone was in front of her, but they were in silhouette, and she could not make out features, only the size. Five-foot eight or nine, athletic build, and that was it. The face was a blank... No, as her eyes adjusted, she could see they wore a mask. Amongst the fear came a sparkle of hope. If she never saw their face, then maybe they would let her live?

That hope died when she saw the knife. It glinted in the subdued light, and the glow seemed to trickle down the serrations until it hit the hilt. It was big, and it was made to tear rather than to cut. If he stuck her with that, then she had no chance. Beneath the ball-gag, she screamed, but all that escaped around its rubber sides was a whimper that sounded like a puppy beaten by its owner.

The knife rose above her and stopped, filling her vision, then it plunged toward her face. Faster and faster it came, she closed her eyes and shrank back into the table. Nothing. Breath held, she waited, and then a breeze touched her face. She opened her eyes. The knife was there just above her, and so was the mask, again the breeze they were blowing onto her, and it caused her spine to spasm and her heart to skip a beat.

The knife withdrew, and she took a breath into aching lungs. Tears formed in her eyes and spilled down her cheeks, but she must not cry, she must stay strong. Again, the knife pulled back, and again, it plunged down. This time it punched her in the shoulder. It felt like her arm went dead, but as the knife withdrew, pain seared through the wound like a red hot poker, and she felt the warm, wet blood spurt out and run down her body. This time the panic took hold and would not give in. She screamed and fought and screamed, but nothing happened. She could not move and could not fight, and again, she was punched. This time in the right side of her stomach. At first, it was a dull pain. Then, the blade was moved in the wound, and she had never felt such agony. Even when her appendix burst, it had been nothing like this.

Madness took her mind, and she rode out the next attack on a wave of delirium. There was no fear, just panic, and insanity, but she could feel weakness now. Loss of blood was slowing her mind, slowing her body. She knew that she had to do something important, but she wanted to hide from the pain. Wanted to sleep and as the knife tore into her gut, she passed out and quietly drifted away as her blood spilled onto the work surface and ran down onto the floor.

The girl let out her last exhalation, and the hunter was filled with euphoria. That death rattle, that breath was almost orgasmic. It made all the weeks of planning and following worthwhile. Tonight had gone quicker than expected. It just showed that it didn't take long to build up skill. There was still a good forty minutes until the sun was up. But the job was not done, one more procedure was necessary the bitch would not be allowed to keep seeing. What was burned on her retinas was not for them, it had to be removed. It had to be kept, preserved, and savored.

The knife felt heavy, it was late, and fatigue was becoming a problem. Still, at the excitement of the task to come, endorphins kicked in, and the job became easier. It was important not to damage the face, so the knife was slipped under the eye and moved around. Slowly cutting away any retaining tissue and then scraped under the eye, it sliced through the optic nerve. Then the eye could be scooped out by the fingers. The leather gloves were not designed for this, and it was messy. Pressure had to be applied, but the eyes must not be damaged. They were important. They were part of the plan.

The first one was pulled out with a sucking sound and dropped into a plastic container. It plopped down and rolled over, so it appeared to be looking back at itself. The next one was harder and squished between the gloves. It took a firm grip and was mashed out of shape, leaking the optic fluid all down the gloves and back into the socket.

Satisfied with the night's work, the lid on the

container was closed, now she must be cleaned and prepared. Nothing must be left to chance, no evidence could be found, and the best way to do that was with a chemical stripping agent that would remove any stray DNA.

CHAPTER ELEVEN

*D*etective Inspector Merlin walked to the crime scene tape, feeling like shit. Sleep had eluded him last night, but that was not the reason for the soul-crushing despair he felt. It was knowing there was another body. Another girl had been tortured, and he had let it happen. If only he had been able to keep Nick Bellamy locked up. Or if he had been able to get a warrant to search his place, then maybe he wouldn't have to see someone's baby carved up like a Christmas dinner.

Mary, the coroner, was already here. She bent over the body, her wiry frame fitter than most people half her age.

"What do we have?" Merlin asked, but he already

knew, and as the older woman stepped to one side, he couldn't prevent the gasp that left him. Like the previous two women, her head was bent back, so she was looking behind her. Once more, the eye sockets were empty, lined with blood which had leaked down like some macabre mascara. It was the only place on the body that the perp left blood. Every other inch would have been cleaned, and as far as they could tell, there was no sexual activity.

He turned to Mary, her short gray hair was neat and tidy, and her eyes sharp, though even she looked a little tired. Maybe this case was getting to the old bird, but he doubted she would ever show it. "Same as all the others?" he asked.

Mary held a small recorder, but she did not need her notes, her memory was fine, and somehow, Merlin thought this one would be etched on it for a long time.

"Too similar to be anyone else," she said. "We have eight wounds in total. I'm not sure if this is significant, that is for you to decide. There is no correlation between organs, as with the other girls, the wounds are placed in a similar configuration but not identical. I haven't turned her over, but there is bruising on her side, so I imagine that we have a blow from behind to the kidney area. There is something I've wondered about the wounds on the other girls. Before, it has never been conclusive, but this time it is. Some of the mutilations were done post mortem, as were the final two wounds. Here." Mary pointed to the long wound down the girl's chest and to the one across her stomach. "In this latter wound, the skin was pulled back to form an opening. I do not believe that was staged, I think it is the beginning of the buildup of decomposition gasses, but of course, I could be wrong."

It's a smile, Merlin thought. *The bastard gave her a smile.*

"You can see the viscera through the wound, just like the other two. That's all I have Detective until I get her back to my lab. Oh." She reached down and picked up an evidence bag. "This was next to the body."

Merlin felt the world stop as she handed him the plastic. Inside was a card, a bloody business card, and the name on it was Nick Bellamy.

Nick sat in the interview room, his stomach churning as he fought that dizzy feeling, the one you get just before you faint. Next to him was a tall man, slightly bald with a bit of a paunch and a suit that looked like it hadn't been pressed for months. He had a lawyer, one Sadie had found for him, but so far, Mr. Craig Wright wasn't filling him with confidence.

Merlin walked in, nodded to both men, and put a folder on the tatty old table. "I want to thank you both for coming in to help us today," he said.

Nick felt his stomach clench, why was he being so nice? This had to be a trap.

"My client is always happy to help the police," Craig said. "Now, perhaps you could enlighten us as to why we are here?"

Merlin opened the file, and Nick felt like he was sucker-punched. The breath left him, his stomach cramped, and he had to fight the vomit that rose in his throat. Luckily he had hardly eaten in the last few days, and there was nothing for his stomach to evacuate. "What...?" Was all he could manage.

Merlin smiled, this was not quite the reaction he wanted, but it would do. The guy obviously didn't like looking at his kills. Curious that, most sickos reveled in it. They would try and hide it, but there was a shortness of breath, a look in their eyes of rapture, but not Nick. Of course, the photo had been of Sara Plimpton after her autopsy.

"Sorry, how did that get in here?" Every time Nick Bellamy saw one of the girls, his reaction was to vomit, why? Shaun's theory that he had a split personality came to mind, so how do I prove it?

Merlin closed the file covering the photo and watched both Nick and Craig breathe a sigh of relief. Both of them had turned a sickly green, and he could tell the lawyer was out of his depth. In fact, they couldn't have been luckier if they had chosen him personally. Craig was well known for his bumbling, and Merlin couldn't remember the last time he had won a case.

"Here, this is the photo I wanted you to look at," Merlin said and pulled a picture of the naked Sara from his file. It was taken from above, and she looked like a porcelain doll floating on the green grass. If not for the wounds and her eyes, it would have been quite an arty shot. "Do you know this girl?"

Nick's face drained of what little color he had left. In fact, he was the shade of a three-day dead corpse, and his mouth opened and closed as his eyes got wider. At last, he found his voice. "How would I know, she... she's... dead?"

Merlin had expected butchered or slaughtered, the word dead didn't fit with this type of killer, it threw him off his game. It was something someone would say in shock. Nick's look, the word was, in fact, what he would expect from an innocent. Nick was not behaving like the hardened killer that Merlin expected. Maybe he was a good actor, or maybe he was two people, and this one knew nothing about the crimes. Then what about this picture? He slid a photocopy of her enlarged drivers' license across to him. It was grainy, but a good likeness.

"Oh God," Nick said. "She looks like..."

"No more questions," Craig butted in. I need to speak to my client alone."

Well, perhaps the lawyer wasn't going to be such a pushover, after all? Merlin nodded and left the room, but he had something. They had noticed all the girls were similar, but then most killers had a type. Yet Nick had intimated that they all looked like someone, so now all he had to do was find out whom.

While the two men colluded, he would find a picture of Nick's wife and any old girlfriend's, of his mom. The business card in the evidence bag made the file weigh a ton. Merlin had thought about using it first to see Nick's reaction, but in the heat of the interview had decided to hold it back. To see what they came up with and then drop the bombshell of the card. Any good lawyer would be able to discount it. Where they found the body was close to Nick's house, and he used the track regularly but, Merlin hoped that Craig would not continue to surprise them.

A quick search on the computer and Nick was able to pull up Sadie Bellamy's driver's license. As the picture came into focus, he could feel the blood rushing in his ears. Could feel the pulse-pounding in his neck. He didn't need to look up any other women, she was a dead ringer for the first victim and very closely matched to the other two. Having seen this picture, it was easier to see the resemblance, and Merlin knew he had him; all he needed now was some solid evidence. There was enough for a warrant, of that he was sure. With a dry throat and a rising sense of urgency, he pulled up the computer form and started filling in the details. It was eight-thirty in the evening if he could find a magistrate then the warrant could be ready in minutes.

Merlin spent the next hour filling in the form and phoning around, trying to get hold of someone to agree to issue the warrant. It was there ready to be emailed over, but so far, he had struck out on finding anyone working. The shift magistrate was Barbara Newman, but she had called in sick. That was one of the frustrations of living in a small town. Nick had kept ringing, all he needed was to get hold of someone who could sign, but every number he tried just rang and rang. It looked like fate was against him.

"Sorry," PC Strike said as he came up to Merlin. "The desk Sergeant says we have to let him go unless you have enough to hold him?"

Merlin felt the bottom drop out of his world, and it took his stomach with it. The card was circumstantial; in fact, everything they had was circumstantial. There was no evidence except that this guy found the first victim, he knew the second and thought the third looked like his wife. It had to be him, but what did he have? Just a business card and a hunch. "Okay, cut him loose and then come back here. I have a job for you."

Merlin was already an hour over his shift, but there was no way he was going home tonight, not until this bastard was locked behind bars, and the women of Donborough could walk home safe again.

PC Strike rushed back all bright-eyed and bushy-tailed, and Merlin handed him a warrant and a list of addresses. "Drive around these, you know the magistrates?"

Strike nodded.

"Great, find me one and get that signed. My mobile number is on the bottom."

Nick drove the car home in a daze. He was out, but the police really believed he was killing those girls. It seemed surreal until you realized how much they looked like Sadie. Would she be home? Why had she lied about last night? Had she lied... maybe he knew nothing about himself and about his wife? All the questions just made him feel so tired. In fact, he was exhausted, yet he had slept half the morning and done nothing all day. Maybe he should go for a run? It was dark and late, but the garage had a treadmill, and maybe his body was tired because he hadn't been training much?

Turning into the drive, a smile crossed his face as he saw the welcoming glow of lights. She was home.

"Hi, Sadie, I'm home," he called.

She rushed through from the kitchen, her face lined with worry. "I've been calling, wondering where you were. Did they really keep you all this time?"

Nick rushed to her and pulled her into his arms and was relieved when she leaned into him, her body soft and comforting. Sometimes she would shove him away when he tried to hug her, but tonight he needed the security to know she was there.

"It was awful," he said. "Three girls have been murdered, brutally murdered. Oh, God Sadie, you would not believe what has been done to them, and the idiot police think I did it because I found the first body. I mean, what idiot killer would report his own kill?"

Sadie chuckled in his ear and then pulled away. "The main thing is you're safe and home. I was really worried about you, and I felt so guilty when the police asked me if you were home all night."

Nick put some distance between them and sat down at the table. "But I was home all night, and since when have you taken sleeping tablets?"

"Always," she said. "I've had a prescription now for over a year. And Nick, you went out last night. I heard the back door and then the back gate open. Now I'm sorry, love, but I have to go to work. There's trouble at the lab."

"Can't you stay a little longer," he asked, cringing at the whiny sound of his own voice. "Maybe we could get a bite to eat?"

Sadie checked her watch and laughed a light sound. "I can sneak half an hour. Sit there, let me get you some toast."

There was a smile on her face, a lightness to her step that Nick had not seen in a while. Who knows, maybe this would do their marriage good? Yet if he were honest, he knew why she was happy, she loved her job, and like a wet weekend, he had backed down and let go of his dreams of children. Part of him wanted to talk to her, to mention it again, but he was so tired it would just have to wait.

She had her back to him and worked busily, buttering the toast. While Nick could not see, her hand slipped into her pocket, and she pulled out a small brown bottle. Taking off the lid, she squeezed two drops into his drink. As she stirred the coffee, she secreted the bottle away before he noticed.

Nick's eyes were closed as a plate was put before him, and the scent of freshly cooked toast drifted between them. Now it was him that was grinning. "Thanks," he said before grabbing hold of the buttery deliciousness and taking a bite.

"My pleasure. You need to eat more I think you've lost weight. I made you a coffee as well. Why not drink it then go for a run?"

Nick nodded, chewing the toast. It felt really good to have food in his stomach, and just maybe he would go for that run. Sadie watched him as he took a drink. They would get through this, and he could wait two years. It was only fair that he gave her that time, and then they would have children. The thought put a smile on his face.

"What?" she asked.

"I just think we can do this. I think we are gonna be alright."

"You bet," she said. "Damn, I left my phone upstairs, back in a minute."

Nick chewed on his toast and sipped the coffee. He was feeling better, more energized, and things were coming into focus. Maybe all he needed was a good sleep and a bit of real food.

Upstairs, Sadie searched behind the sink. *Where was it?* The problem was Nick was a bit of a slob, and he left his comb everywhere. She checked the bathroom window, the hall window ledge, and finally found it in the bedroom. She was in luck. Three hairs were sticking out of the comb. Taking a plastic bag from her pocket, she deposited the hairs and tucked the bag back out of the way. Now all she needed was a final victim. The cops had been so stupid they hadn't put things together yet. She had left clues all over the house. The mud on his shoes and beneath his nails was blood and mud, and even though he had cleaned them, she was sure that traces would remain. Obviously, she had to be a bit more direct. The business card, the look of the girls, if only they had got a warrant they would find the evidence she had planted on his laptop. They didn't know he never used it. She had made sure that she had visited some pretty hardcore sites and done all her research on the girls on it. Still, her plan could still work. All she needed was another victim. As she skipped down the stairs, she scoured her mind for women who looked even remotely like her. The problem was it had taken her a long time to find these three. Finding more would be impossible, it would take too long.

He smiled up at her as she rounded the corner, and every cell in her body wanted to lash out and just rip off his head. That would not do. Instead, she smiled. "Got it," she said. "Now I really have to go. Why not go to bed? You look exhausted, get some sleep, and I will see you in the morning."

Nick smiled. "I think I will. Sadie, thank you."

She pecked him on the cheek, picked up her gym bag, and walked to the door. It was dark and unwelcoming outside, but she did not mind the cold.

Closing the door, she noticed light bounce off a car across the road. It was not one from the neighborhood, and it piqued her interest. Maybe she had just found her victim?

She backed her Audi out of the drive, and using her reversing camera, she took the number plate. Her memory was good, and she could look it up from the lab. Computers were easy if you knew how to coax them. Pretending to be concentrating, she drove past the car. A man was leaning back, hoping that the shadows hid him; he was tall with short brown hair shaved close to his head. A thought crossed her mind, and as she drove on, a smile beamed from her face.

Sadie pecked Nick on the cheek, and he watched as she picked up her gym bag and walked to the door. As it closed behind her, Nick let his head drop to the table, and tears ran from his eyes and dripped onto the wood.

This was getting him nowhere. Sitting up, he fought down the pity party. Things were happening around him, and he had to work out if he was involved. Should he call the police and tell them about his lost time? Tell them about his muddy footprints? No, he should start from the beginning. Sadie was standing by him, supporting him. It felt good, he would not let her down.

Yet still, he didn't know what was happening to him? A deep fear had started to grow in his gut, and he could feel the roots as they wheedled their way through his intestines and dug themselves into his very soul. When every one of the girls had been killed, he was asleep. That was explainable. It was night, late, and where else would he be. The problem was, the following morning, his trainers were covered in mud, and it was tracked all over the carpet. Could he be the killer?

A wave of sickness rolled over him, and he had to fight down the toast as it erupted from his stomach. Taking another sip of coffee, he bit it back and tried to think. How could he prove he was home? Another thought started in his mind. Why had Sadie not chewed his balls off for the mud on the carpet? She was a neat freak, hated anything out of order. If he came into the kitchen wearing his trainers, she had a fit. 'That's what a mudroom is for,' was one of her favorite sayings.

Another thought started deep down in his gut, and this one filled him with stone-cold dread and the spark of a burgeoning excitement. He threw away his coffee and found out the video camera. Setting it up before the bone-breaking fatigue took him down to God knows where he felt more confident than he had in years. Tomorrow morning he would know.

Outside the Bellamy's house, Merlin sat in his car. It was tucked beneath a tree, and he was sure he was in shadow when he saw Sadie Bellamy leave. She was dressed in a dark business suit and carrying a bag. For a second, he contemplated following her, but no, he was best to keep his eye on Nick, and he knew from his research that she often worked late.

Her Audi reversed out of the drive and towards his car. Closer and closer it came, and he felt himself twitch with the urge to move backward. Just before she hit him, she stopped, turned the wheel, and then did an exaggerated U-turn back past him. He shrank back against the seat, sure that she would not spot him but not wanting to take a chance. As her taillights disappeared from his rearview mirror, he wondered if she had not been driving long. Or maybe it was a new car because if she had that much trouble backing out her drive every night, then maybe she needed some lessons.

Bringing his mind back to the house, Merlin settled in for the night. Maybe he should have made this official, got back up, as there was a gate behind the property. The problem was his boss was not as sure about Nick being guilty, and if he made it official and got told to go home, then it made things tricky.

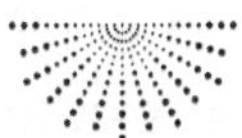

CHAPTER THIRTEEN

Sadie drove past her lab and around the corner to a series of lock-ups. She pulled up at number six and got out of the car. In the small neat space was a closet, a desk, chair, and a small sofa. A door opened into a shower room, which she would need later, and down one side, there were a number of plastic containers all bearing a hazard sign.

Quickly she changed into a black skin-tight boiler suit and tied back her hair. From one of the containers, she squirted liquid into her hand and rubbed it over her face, neck, and hands. It was a sealant and would prevent any DNA or stay hairs being left at the scene. Of course, if they did find anything from her, they would assume it was contamination from Nick.

Grabbing her bag, she took a quick look around and left. Everything was in place. She had been having therapy sessions for over a month now. Telling how Nick kept asking if she would die for him, and she had made sure that her arms were covered in bruises. That wasn't hard. All she had to do was let the men at her MMA classes win for once.

Leaving the lock-up, she walked a short way and got into a small white van. The plates were false, and she changed them regularly. It was unregistered and impossible to trace. Excitement made her breath catch in her throat, and her heart raced against her ribs. This was it, the perfect end to her project, and more than that, the chemical worked. It was tasteless, undetectable, and given time it would kill. Of course, the client didn't want death, they just needed to incapacitate, and for that, it worked a treat.

A smile crossed her face as she remembered the look on the client's face when she said that human testing was already underway and that the results were promising. They had been more than promising; the drug had worked a treat. Nick remembered nothing she did to him. One night she had changed his clothes, dragged him downstairs, and left him on the sofa. Through the whole thing, he never stirred, and in the morning, he thought that he had dropped to sleep where he woke. Another time, quite early into the experiment, she had pulled down his pajamas and taken his limp dick in her mouth. Slowly she had teased the beast to an erection, yet his eyes never opened. Sitting astride him, she rode him hard, and then with him inside her, she had fingered herself to an orgasm and screamed out his name. All the time, his breathing remained calm, his eyes closed, and he never even stirred. She had fallen asleep with her head on his shoulder, a smile on her face. It was working.

She was close, just one street away from home. Pulling the van up next to the local shop, she decided to walk the rest of the way. Stepping out onto the deserted street, a cold wind plastered her clothes to her body, and a thin drizzle started. It was not the nicest of nights, but her thoughts kept her warm.

It had been only an hour since she left the house, and there was still the possibility of someone on the street. So, with caution, she kept to the shadows and took a ginnel that skirted the back of the properties and should bring her up close behind the policeman's car.

As a hunter, she moved silently, slipping from shadow to shadow. Every nerve in her body was alert as she approached the car. It looked like the copper had fallen asleep. His head was against the car's door pillar, and he had not moved for over a minute. Like a shadow, she stepped up to the car and almost let out a gasp of delight. The fool had left the doors unlocked.

Her hand found the cold metal as blood rushed through her ears. Taking a breath, she steadied herself. This next step must be one silent, fluid movement, or else all was lost. Letting out the breath, she lifted the handle, pulled the door, and slipped into the back of the car. Her hand was poised next to his throat, the serrated hunting knife ready to deal out death if he moved.

Luck was on her side, the Detective slept on, and Sadie had time to decide how to do this. On the drive over, she had wondered whether to simply kill the man or whether to transform him as she had done the girls. Of course, the planning was not the same, and she would be unable to do her best work from the back seat of a car.

From her bag, she pulled out a cloth, the chemical formula was her own. Barely detectable, it put her victims into a deep sleep, but it left a terrible hangover. That was one problem she had been unable to iron out, but considering how she used the drug, it did not matter. When her victims woke, the least of their problems was the hangover.

A car turned onto the street, and the lights snaked across them, blinding Sadie for a moment. She ducked down as the Detective stirred. This was not good; to be caught now would ruin all her plans. The car turned a corner and was gone, but the man in front of her sat more upright. Sadie held her breath. Would he fall back to sleep, would he decide to go home or would he stay awake and maybe discover her hiding behind him? If she moved, he might feel her or see a shadow, so she crouched down low and prayed that her muscles would not cramp.

Gradually she heard his breathing slow, and bit by bit, she moved back into position. Sitting upright, she freed her cutting arm and brought the knife around in front of the man. Just before she made the killer blow, she heard a sharp intake of breath. She was caught. His hands came up, but she was too quick, and she pulled the blade down. The metal bit into his fingers and hesitated as it touched bone. The fool was fighting her, and as he pushed the knife, it slipped, cutting off chunks of flesh from his fingers. They fell into his lap while he swore and cursed. There was desperation in his voice as if he already knew he was dead, and then the blade was free, and it dug into his throat.

Sadie recognized the difference in skin texture and yanked the blade towards her. It sliced through flesh and cartilage, his hands dropping away as his life burbled out of his esophagus along with his blood. Frenzied now, she pulled back even harder, her hands slipped, and the slick feel of the blood and the flesh was astonishing. No matter how often she cut into the soft tissue of another human being, it was always new, always orgasmic in its intensity. The knife hit bone, and a laugh escaped her. It was perfect.

Leaning into the passenger seat and with practiced ease, she cut out both of his eyes. There was a plan for those too. Nick never went into their shed, yet she had taken her time and made it look like his den.

Over a month ago, using his credit card, she had bought and installed a small fridge. In it was a plastic container that held the eyes of all the victims. It had not taken her long to get a tub, which bore his fingerprints.

Everything was perfect. Sadie took out a plastic bag from earlier and carefully placed Nick's hair on the headrest where she sat. Then she slipped from the car. All she had to do now was get cleaned up, get to work, and alter the logs to make it look like she had been there all night. They say the perfect murder is impossible, but not only had she committed the perfect murder once but four times, and in the process, she had also got rid of her husband.

CHAPTER FOURTEEN

$\mathcal{N}$ick had woken to the sound of knocking at his door. It was the police, and as he had suspected, they had brought him into the station. That had been over an hour ago. Fear and worry could hardly penetrate the fog and exhaustion he felt. Part of him welcomed what was to come, it had to be over. He had declined a lawyer and was waiting for them to talk to him, but so far, no one came to see him.

At last, the door opened, and an older man walked in. At around five foot nine, with graying hair and a face that could make him your favorite uncle, this was not someone that Nick recognized. There was something about the man, a hardness that his face denied. With a catch of his breath, Nick worked out what it was. The man was in shock.

"I want to talk to Detective Inspector Merlin," Nick said, but the words died in his throat as the man turned to face him, his face tense his eyes hard. Something was wrong, something was terribly wrong.

"Well, you will have to talk to me instead. I'm Sargent Brookes," the man said, pulling out a seat and sitting down as if the world was too heavy and he needed to rest. "I believe you have waived your right to legal representation, is that correct?"

"Yes," Nick said. "I sent an email last night. I think…"

Brookes cut him off with a wave of the hand. "I think it's a little late for confessions. Why did you kill Detective Inspector Merlin?"

"What?"

Question after question was fired at Nick, and soon, he was so confused that all he could do was sit back and take it. Merlin had been killed outside his house, and apparently, there was evidence linking him to the crime. This time there was no sickness, just the cold reality that she had framed him. Now he understood what had been going on. The lost time, the exhaustion, Sadie making his electrolyte drink. With Merlin gone, they would not find the email or the camera, and Sadie would get away with murder. Despite the pressure and the constant barrage of questions, Nick felt the exhaustion take over, and he nodded as he let out a yawn. A slap on the table jerked him back to the present.

"Keeping you awake, are we?" Brookes asked.

"There's something wrong with me. Look I understand how you feel, just do me one favor, check Merlin's email." Nick finished, but he was finding it so hard to concentrate that he had no idea if he had said the right things, and as they booked him, it was all a blur. As soon as he was shoved into the cell, he sank down and fell asleep.

Brookes booked the guy and walked back to his desk. It all seemed too easy. Why had he killed the detective and why had he suddenly left evidence. Merlin had been a good cop, and it pained Michael to see him go out this way. His throat cut, and his eyes sliced from his face. But everything pointed to Bellamy, and Brookes was about to leave it, to move on when a nagging voice in the back of his mind started. *When was a case ever this perfect?* With a growing buzz in his stomach, he made a quick call to PC Sam Strike. The youngster was a whizz with computers, and then he made the journey down to the morgue, for a conversation with Mary.

Two hours later, Brookes had what he needed, and now all he had to do was book the killer and then give the bad news. Relatives were always the hardest part of the job, whether it was the heart-wrenching job of telling them of a lost loved one or telling them that their partner was a murderer. Still, it had to be done. Somehow he knew this time would not be easy.

Michael walked down the tired gray corridor, his leather shoes slapping on the hard floor. The interview room would be set up as he requested, and he entered to find Mrs. Bellamy sat to attention. The room contained a table, two chairs, a television, and a DVD player. She was facing the two-way mirror. Her face was neutral, which made her either a good actor or an uncaring bitch.

Michael sat down at the nondescript table. "I want to thank you for coming in. Do you know what this is all about?" he asked. Now there was emotion, Sadie's lip quivered, and she lowered her eyes.

"Is it Nick?" she asked.

Michael nodded. "Yes. We arrested him earlier for the murder of three women and a police officer."

"Oh my God," she said.

There was shock on her face, but Michael was sure that her eyes were too bright, the curve of her lips wrong. This was one cold-hearted bitch.

"Of course, we now have new information. It appears that your husband is innocent, but then, of course, you know that, don't you?" Michael watched as the smile slipped off her face, and then he pressed play on the remote control on the table.

On the screen, they watched as she walked into her house, straight past Nick, who slept on the couch. Dropping the bag on the kitchen floor as always, she put her clothes straight into the washing machine and switched it on. Then she pulled a container from her bag. She lifted it to her face and opened the lid, and then with a smile, she wandered over to Nick. Touching something in the box, she withdrew her fingers and looked at them. With a smile, she wiped her fingers on his, and then she sat and whispered into his ear.

"That goes on for quite a while," Brookes said. "We guess you are telling him what he did, maybe that confuses him, who knows?"

Her head was still held high, and there was defiance in her eyes.

On the tape, she looked into the box and smiled the sickest smile Brookes had ever seen. Then she stood, unlocked the back door, and walked out of the house.

"We found your husband's den, which funnily enough had very little of his DNA and none of his fingerprints. We found the fridge with the tub and its contents. It may take us a while, but we will find how you did this. Your husband never left that room from before Detective Inspector Merlin died. So, Mrs. Bellamy, you are under arrest.

It was three weeks before Nick started to feel like himself again. Blood tests showed nothing wrong, but they had found a small bottle in Sadie's clothes. So far, no one knew what it was. He was no longer weak and no longer falling asleep all the time. Things should have been good, but guilt and despair filled him in equal portions.

Nightmares haunted his sleep. In them, he was the hunter he stalked women. Their hair color no longer mattered as he followed them, breath held, heart-pounding he knew he had a solution. They would all look like Sadie. There was heaven and hell in the hunt. Creeping up on them, closer and closer while they were blissfully unaware. Guilt made him want to shout out, but something held him back. The day times were a world of misery, betrayal, and guilt. The only time he felt whole was when he stuck the knife into their back and felt their blood warm and suggestive as it ran over his hand.

Every morning, when he woke, the first thing he saw was a box of blonde wigs. He had bought them online but did not remember doing it. He wondered then if he should hand himself in, but so far there had been no mud on the carpet, so far there had been no murders, so far it was only a dream.

25th April 1582

The basement of the cage.

Derbyshire.

England.

3:15 am.

Alden Carter looked down at his shaking hands. The sight of blood curdled his stomach as it dripped onto the floor. For a moment, his resolve failed, he did not recognize the thin, gnarled fingers. Did not recognize the person he had become. How could he do this, how could he treat another human being in this terrible way and yet he knew he must. If he did not, then the consequences for him would be grave. For a second he imagined a young girl with a thin face and a long nose. Her brown hair bounced as she ran in circles and she flashed a smile each time she passed. The memory brought him joy and comfort. Brook was not a pretty girl, but she was his daughter, and he loved her more than he could say. He remembered her joy at the silver cross he gave her. The one that he was given from the Bishop, the one that cost him his soul.

Rubbing his hands through sparse hair, he almost gagged at the feeling of the crusty blood he found there. How many times had he run those blood-soaked fingers through his lank and greasy hair? Too many to count. It had been a long night, and it was not over yet. This must be done, and it was him who had to do it.

Suddenly, his throat was dry, and fatigue weighed him down like the black specter of death he had become. A candle flickered and cast a grotesque shadow across the wall. Outside, the trees shook their skeletal fingers against the brick and wood house and he closed his eyes for a moment. Seeing Brook once more he strengthened his resolve. The trees trembled, and the wind seemed to whisper through their leaves, tormenting him, telling him that he was wrong but he would not stop. Could not stop. Taking a breath, he felt stronger now, and with a shaky hand, he picked up an old stein and took a drink of bitter ale. It did not quench his thirst, but it gave him a little courage. He must do this. He must go back down to the cage and finish what he had started, for if he did not Brook would not survive and maybe neither would he?

The kitchen was sparse and dark and yet he knew he was lucky. The house was made of brick as well as wood. It was three stories' high and was bigger than he needed. This was a luxury few could afford. As was the plentiful supply of food in the pantry and work every day. The Bishop had been kind to him, and he knew he had much to be grateful for. Yet, what price had he paid? As the wind picked up, the trees got angry and seemed to curse him with their branches. Rattling against the walls and making ghostly shadows through the window. Alden turned from them and up to the wall before him. The sight of it almost stopped his heart and yet he knows he must go back down to the cage. If the Bishop found him up here with his job not done, then he would be in trouble... Brook would be in trouble. A shiver ran down his spine as he approached the secret door. Reaching out a shaky hand he touched the wall. It was cold, hard and yet it gave before him. With a push, the catch released and the door swung inward. Before him was a dark empty space. A chasm, an evil pit that he must descend into once more.

Picking up the oil lamp, he approached the stairs and slowly walked down into the dark. The walls were covered in whitewash, and yet they did not seem light. Nothing about this place seemed light. Shadows chased across the ceiling behind him and then raced in front as if eager to reach the hell below. Cobwebs clawed at his face. These did not bother Alden, he did not fear the spider, no, it was the serpent in God's clothing who terrified him.

With each step, the temperature dropped. He had never understood why it was so much colder down here. Cellars were always cool, but this one... with each step, he felt as if he was falling into the lake. That he had broken through the ice and was sinking into the water. Panic clenched his stomach as he wondered if he would drown. The air seemed to stagnate in his lungs, and they ached as he tried to pull in a breath. It was just panic, he shook it off, and was back on the stairs. His feet firm on the stone steps he descended deeper and deeper. He shrugged into his thick, coarse jacket. The material would not protect him, of that he was sure, but he pushed such thoughts to the back of his mind and stepped onto the soft soil of the basement floor.

There was an old wooden table to his right. Quickly, he put the oil lamp on it. Shadows chased across the room. In front of him, his work area was just touched with the light, he knew he must look confident as he approached the woman shackled to the wall. Ursula Kemp was once a beauty. With red hair and deep green eyes. Her smooth ivory skin was traced with freckles, and she had always worn a smile that had the local men bowing to her every need. Seven years ago she had married the blacksmith, and they had a daughter, Rose. Alden felt his eyes pulled to his right... there in the shadows lay a pile of bones. A small pile, the empty eyes of the skull accused him. Though he could not look away from that blackened, burned, mound... the cause of another stain on his soul. Bile rose in his throat, and the air seemed full of smoke. It was just his imagination, he swallowed, choked down a cough and pulled his eyes away.

Blinking back tears, he turned and looked up at Ursula. Chained to the wall she should be beaten, broken, and yet there was defiance in her eyes. They were like a cool stream on a hot summer's day. Something about them defied the position she was in. How could she not be beaten? How could she not confess?

"Confess witch," he said the words with more force than he felt. Fear and anger fired his speech and maybe just a little shame. "Confess, and this will be over."

Ursula's eyes stared back at him cool, calm, unmoving. She looked across at the bones, and he expected her to break. Yet her face was calm... her lips twitched into a smile.

Alden's eyes followed hers. The bones were barely visible in the dark, but he could still see them as clear as day. A glint of something sparkled in the lamplight, but he did not see it. All he could see was the bones. Sweat formed on his palms as if his hands remembered putting them there. Remembered how they felt, strangely smooth and powdery beneath his fingers. *Ash is like silk on the fingers...* a sob almost escaped him, and for a second he wanted to free

Ursula, to tell her to run... and yet, if he did then the Bishop may turn him and Brook into a heap of ash like the one he was trying to not look at.

In his mind, he heard the sound of a screaming child, the sound of the flames. Smelt the burning, an almost tantalizing scent of roasting meat. Shaking his head, he pushed the thoughts away. Now was the time for strength. Biting down on his lip, he fought back the tears and turned to face her once more.

"You will not break me," she shouted defiantly. "Unlike you, I have done no wrong. Kill me, and I will haunt you and your family until the end of time."

Alden turned as anger overrode his judgment, striding to the table he picked up a knife. It was thin, cruel, and the blade glinted in the lamplight. Controlling the shaking of his hands, he crossed the room and plunged it into her side. For a second it caught... stopped by the thickness of her skin. Controlled by rage, he leaned all his strength against it and it sliced into her. Slick, warm blood poured across his fingers. "Confess, confess NOW," he screamed spraying her face with spittle.

A noise from above set his heart beating at such a rate that he thought she must hear it. It pounded in his chest and reminded him of his favorite horse as it galloped across the fields.

The Bishop was here.

Without a confession, he was damned, but maybe he was damned anyway. Maybe his actions doomed him to never rest, yet he must save his daughter, he must save his darling Brook.

As he heard the door above open, panic filled his mind, he must act now, or it would be too late. Then he saw it in her eyes, Ursula knew what was coming. She knew she would die soon and yet she did not fear it. Maybe she thought she would meet her daughter, that they would be together again. He did not know, but the calm serenity in her eyes chilled him to the bone.

In a fit of rage, he struck her on the temple. The light left her eyes, her head dropped forward, and she was unconscious, but it no longer mattered... he had a plan.

"You have confessed," he shouted. "You are a witch.

By the power of the church, I sentence you to death, you will be hung by the neck until you die."

Before the Bishop reached him, he pulled back his hand and slapped her hard across the face. The slap did not wake her, but the noise resounded across the cellar. As the Bishop stopped behind him, he felt an even deeper chill. This man had no morals, no conscience. Alden knew what he had done was wrong, but he did not care. If it kept his family safe, he would sacrifice any number of innocents, and yet his stomach turned at the thought of what was to come.

"You have your confession," the Bishop's voice was harsh in the darkness. "Let us hang her and end this terrible business."

Ursula woke to the feel of rough, coarse hemp around her neck. As her eyes came open, she felt the pain in her side and knew it was a mortal wound. The agony of it masked the multiple injuries she had received over the past few days.

Alden was holding her. Hoisting her up onto a

platform which was suspended over the rail of the balcony. The rope tightened as he placed her feet on the smooth wood and fear filled her. This was it, she knew what was coming, and yet she shook the fear away. To her side, the Bishop stood, a lace handkerchief in his hand as he dabbed at the powder on his face. Blond hair covered a plump but handsome visage, with good bones and a wide mouth, but his eyes... they were gray and hard. The color of a gravestone they could cut through granite with just a look. Amusement danced in them, or maybe it was just the lamp flickering. It could not provide nearly enough light for her to really tell, and yet she knew.

Alden moved away from her and turned to the Bishop. There was a hardness to him too. His lips were drawn tight enough to make a thin line, but he could not fool her. Alden was afraid, and she pitied him, pitied the days to come. For her, it was over. Death would be a sweet release, but for Alden, it had only just begun. As he pushed the table, she looked down to the floor below. The lamp did not light more than half way, and it seemed that she would jump into a bottomless pit. If the rope did not stop her... then maybe she could fly. Down deep she hoped she would soar, away from pain, away from fear and safe in the knowledge she held.

If only.

The moon came from behind a cloud and shone through the window at her back. Its light cast shadows through the branches of a large, old oak tree. Sketchy fingers coalesced on the far wall, and her heart pounded in her chest.

Was this a sign?

A welcome?

The shadows danced and then formed and appeared to be a finger pointing to her doom.

It was time.

Before Alden could push her, she stepped out into nothing.

Get the 4 novel box set Don't Close Your Eyes for free with Kindle Unlimited or just 0.99 for a limited time.

4 TERRIFYING
HAUNTED HOUSE NOVELS
Don't
CLOSE
your
EYES
CAROLINE CLARK
BRYNLEE HOUSE
SHADOW HILL HOUSE
DON'T KILL YOU
BEHIND YOU

The Ghosts of RedRise House 4 book Box Set:

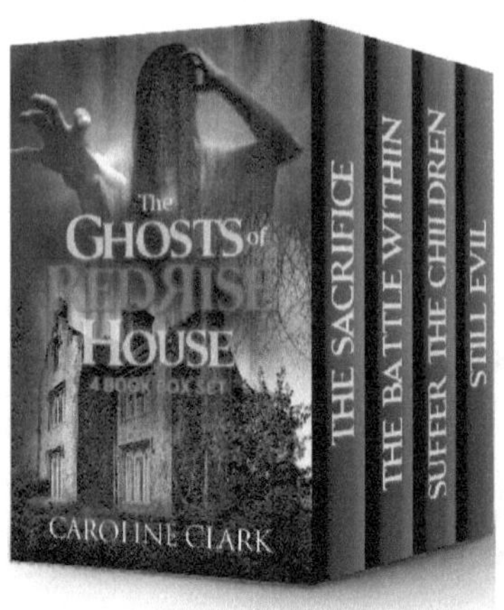

Standalone Books

The Haunting of the Old Box

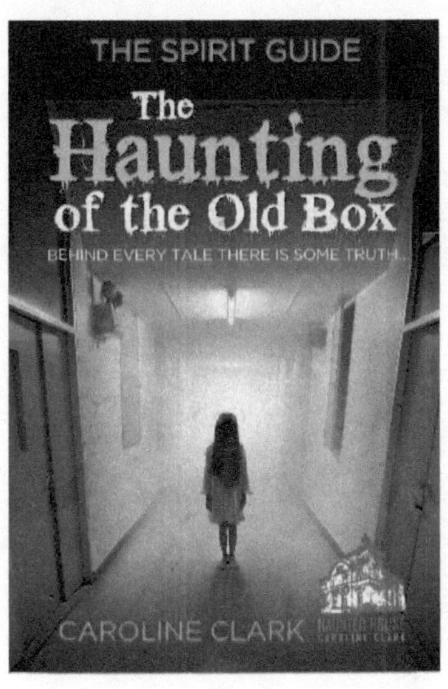

Find all my books USA http://amzn.to/2yYL9Pz

UK http://amzn.to/2z0W1MH

**Subscribe to Caroline Clark's newsletter
for new release announcements
and occasional free content:
http://eepurl.com/cGdNvX**

Caroline Clark is a British author who has always loved the macabre, the spooky, and anything that goes bump in the night.

She was brought up on stories from James Herbert, Shaun Hutson, and many more. Even at school, she was always living in her stories and was often asked to read them out in front of the class. Her teachers didn't always appreciate her more sinister tales.

Now she spends her time researching haunted houses or imagining what must go on in them. These tales then get written up and become her books.

Caroline lives in Lincolnshire with her two boxer dogs. Of course, one of them is called Spooky.

You can contact Caroline via her Facebook page: https://www.facebook.com/CarolineClarkAuthor/

Via her newsletter: http://eepurl.com/cGdNvX

Or on CazClark.com

She loves to hear from her readers.

Why not follow her on Amazon

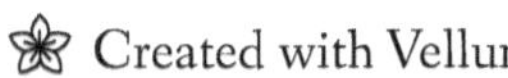 Created with Vellum